DISNEP
PIRATES of the CARIBBEAN

DEAD MEN TELL NO TALES

MOVIE GRAPHIC NOVEL

JOE BOOKS LTD

"I always leave ONE MAN ALIVE to tell the TALE."

—Captain Salaza

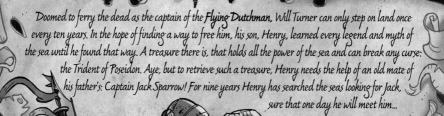

Doomed to ferry the dead as the captain of the *Flying Dutchman*, Will Turner can only step on land once every ten years. In the hope of finding a way to free him, his son, Henry, learned every legend and myth of the sea until he found that way. A treasure there is, that holds all the power of the sea and can break any curse: the Trident of Poseidon. Aye, but to retrieve such a treasure, Henry needs the help of an old mate of his father's: Captain Jack Sparrow! For nine years Henry has searched the seas looking for Jack, sure that one day he will meet him...

1751. HENRY TURNER IS ABOARD THE MONARCH, A BRITISH WARSHIP...

FASTER, YOU PATHETIC BILGE RATS! WE'RE CHASING DOWN PIRATES!

!

HENRY...GET BACK HERE! YOU DON'T WANT TO BE KICKED OFF ANOTHER SHIP!

I HAVE TO SPEAK TO THE CAPTAIN! BE RIGHT BACK, SIR!

MY GOD...

TURNER!!!

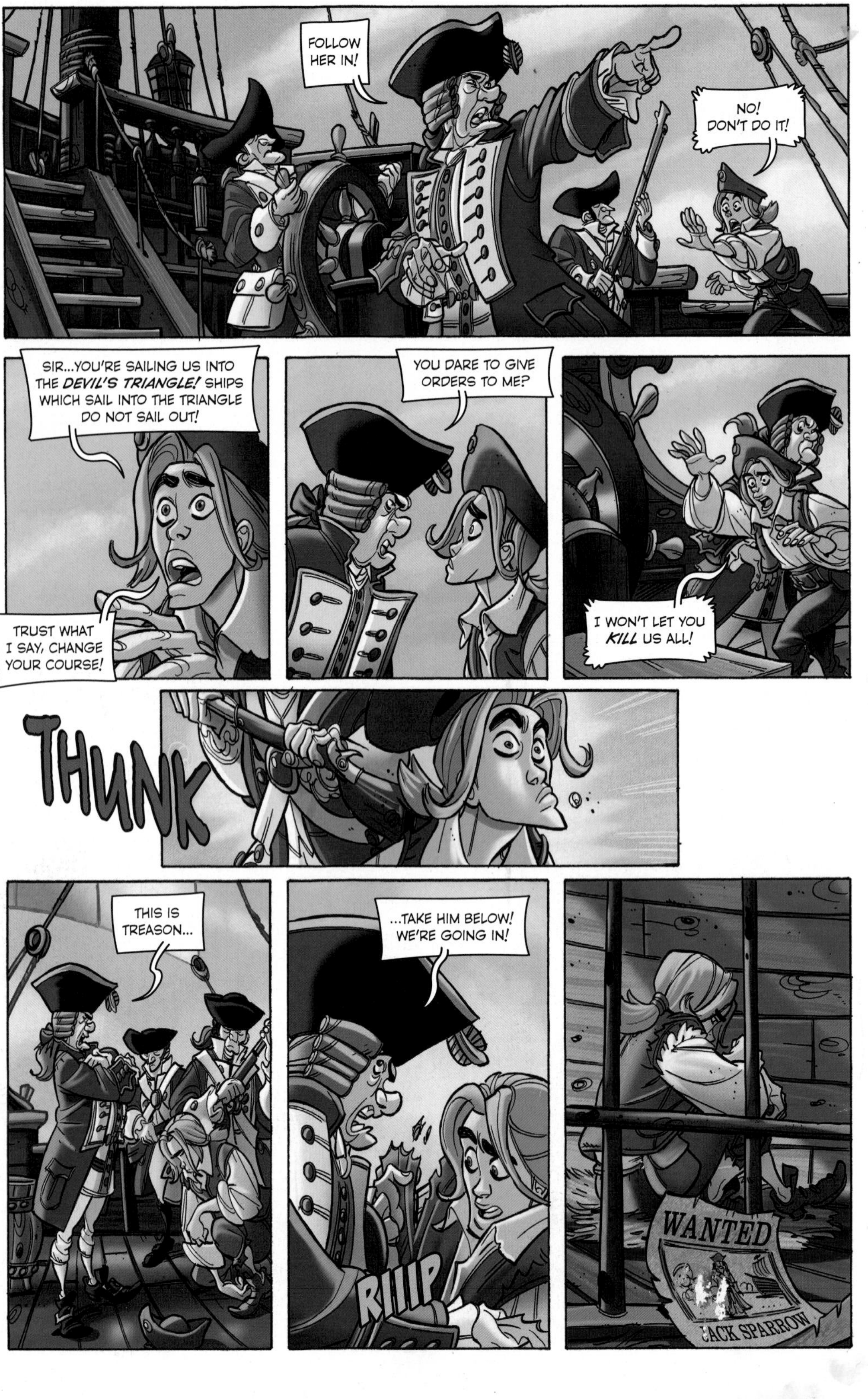

FOLLOW HER IN!
NO! DON'T DO IT!
SIR...YOU'RE SAILING US INTO THE DEVIL'S TRIANGLE! SHIPS WHICH SAIL INTO THE TRIANGLE DO NOT SAIL OUT!
TRUST WHAT I SAY, CHANGE YOUR COURSE!
YOU DARE TO GIVE ORDERS TO ME?
I WON'T LET YOU KILL US ALL!
THUNK
THIS IS TREASON...
...TAKE HIM BELOW! WE'RE GOING IN!
RIIIP
WANTED
ACK SPARROW

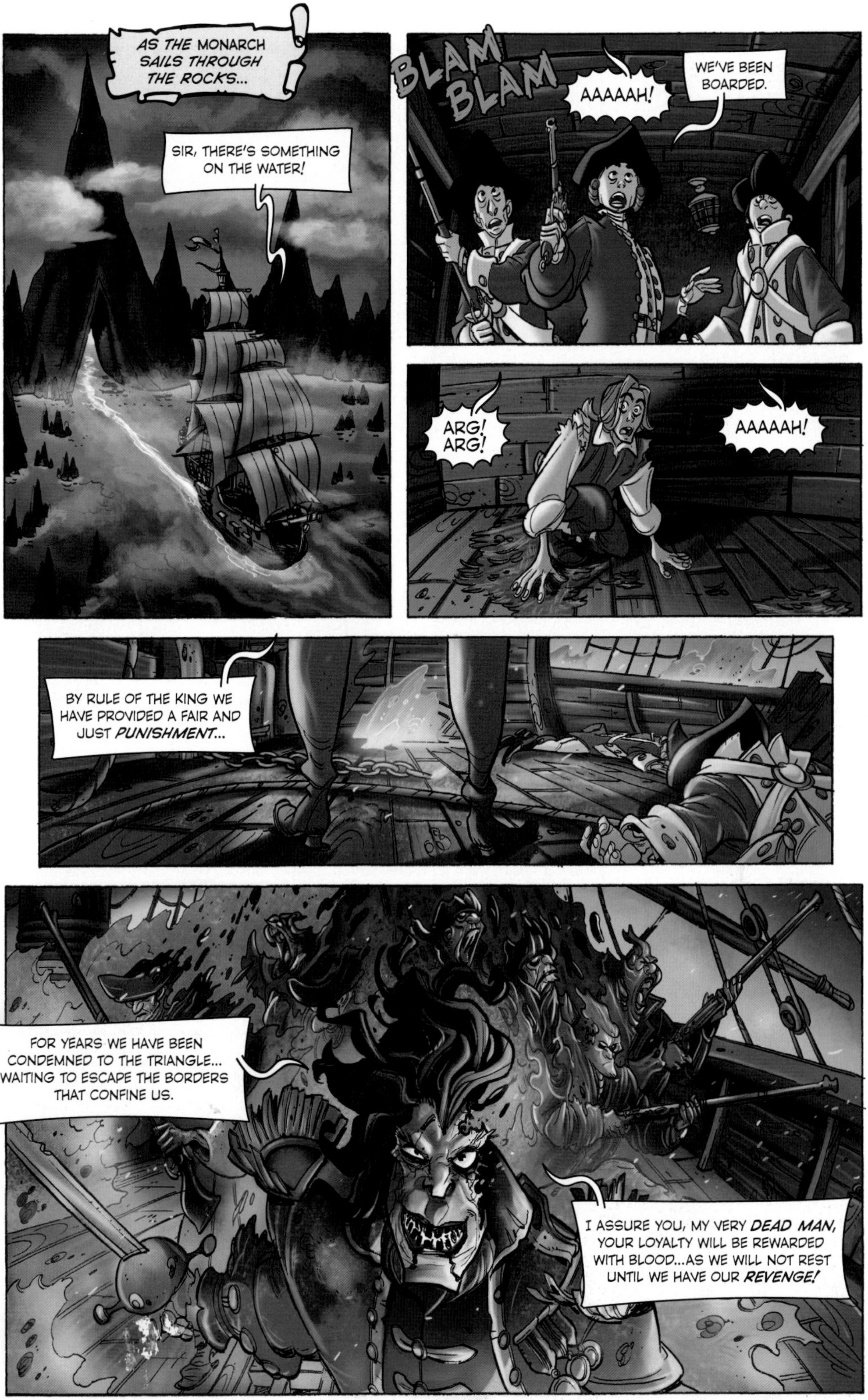
AS THE MONARCH SAILS THROUGH THE ROCKS...
SIR, THERE'S SOMETHING ON THE WATER!
BLAM BLAM
AAAAAH!
WE'VE BEEN BOARDED.
ARG! ARG!
AAAAAH!
BY RULE OF THE KING WE HAVE PROVIDED A FAIR AND JUST PUNISHMENT...
FOR YEARS WE HAVE BEEN CONDEMNED TO THE TRIANGLE... WAITING TO ESCAPE THE BORDERS THAT CONFINE US.
I ASSURE YOU, MY VERY DEAD MAN, YOUR LOYALTY WILL BE REWARDED WITH BLOOD...AS WE WILL NOT REST UNTIL WE HAVE OUR REVENGE!

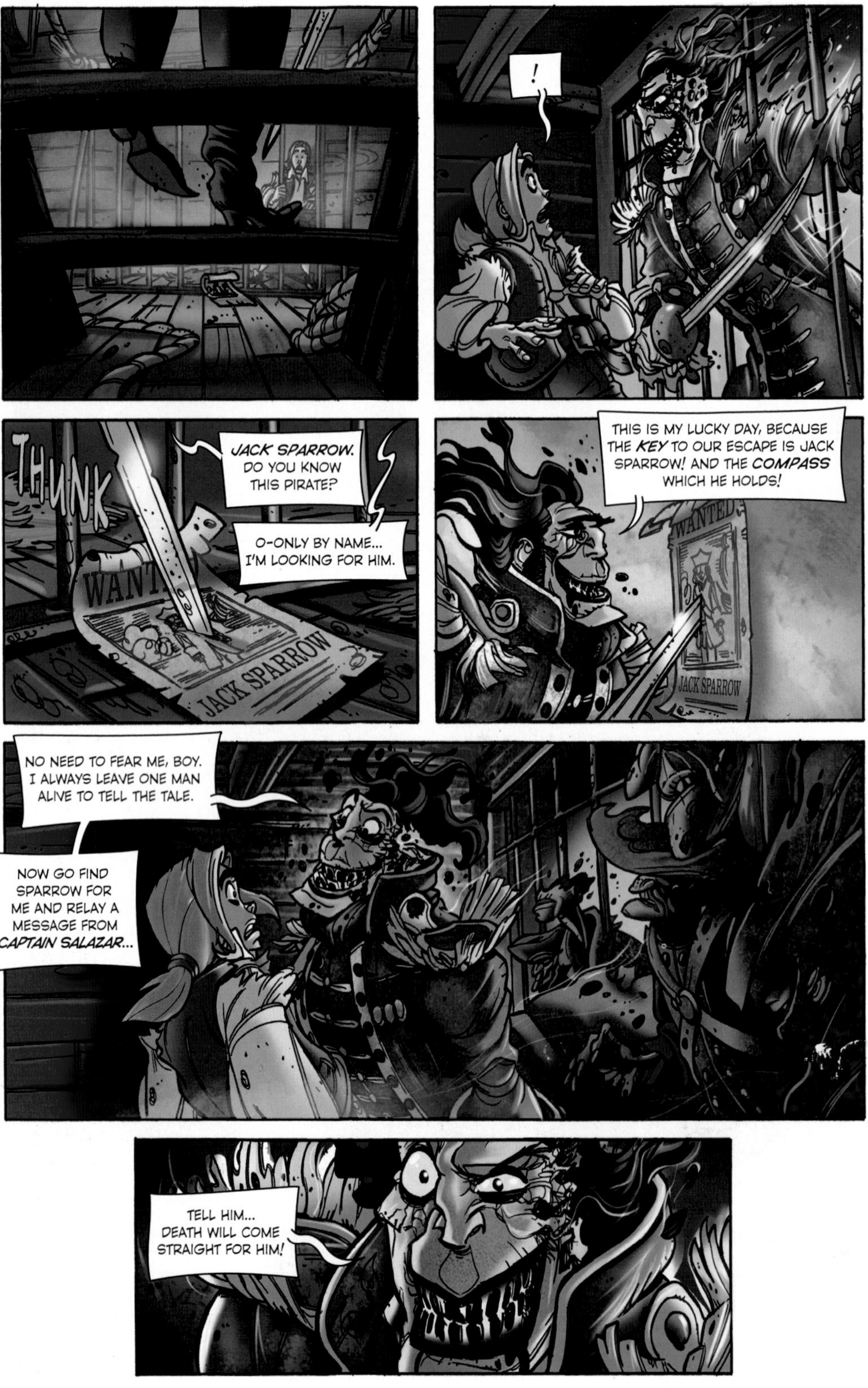
!
THUNK
JACK SPARROW. DO YOU KNOW THIS PIRATE?
O-ONLY BY NAME... I'M LOOKING FOR HIM.
WANTED
JACK SPARROW
THIS IS MY LUCKY DAY, BECAUSE THE KEY TO OUR ESCAPE IS JACK SPARROW! AND THE COMPASS WHICH HE HOLDS!
WANTED
JACK SPARROW
NO NEED TO FEAR ME, BOY. I ALWAYS LEAVE ONE MAN ALIVE TO TELL THE TALE.
NOW GO FIND SPARROW FOR ME AND RELAY A MESSAGE FROM CAPTAIN SALAZAR...
TELL HIM... DEATH WILL COME STRAIGHT FOR HIM!

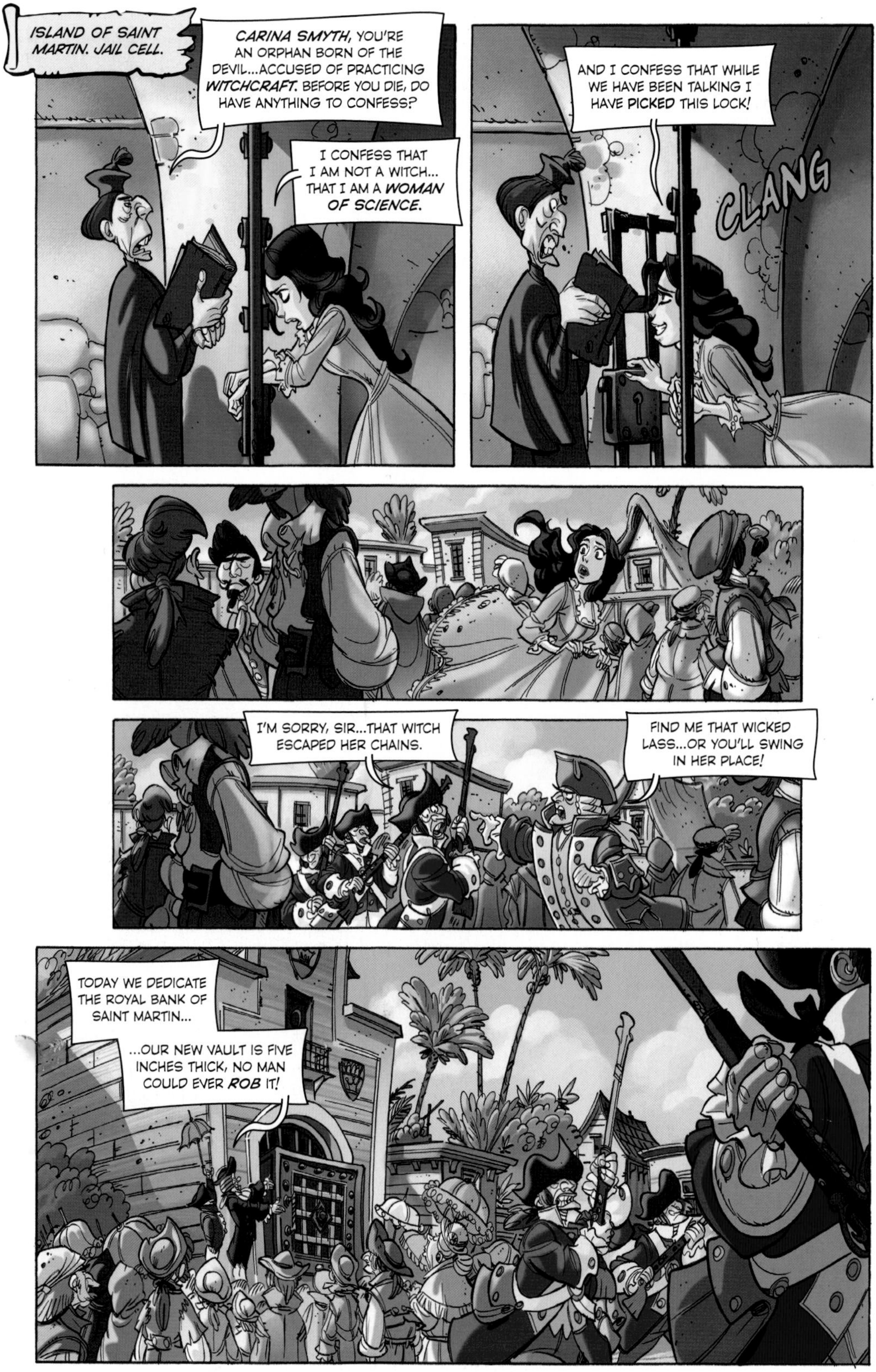
ISLAND OF SAINT MARTIN. JAIL CELL.
CARINA SMYTH, YOU'RE AN ORPHAN BORN OF THE DEVIL...ACCUSED OF PRACTICING WITCHCRAFT. BEFORE YOU DIE, DO HAVE ANYTHING TO CONFESS?
I CONFESS THAT I AM NOT A WITCH... THAT I AM A WOMAN OF SCIENCE.
AND I CONFESS THAT WHILE WE HAVE BEEN TALKING I HAVE PICKED THIS LOCK!
CLANG
I'M SORRY, SIR...THAT WITCH ESCAPED HER CHAINS.
FIND ME THAT WICKED LASS...OR YOU'LL SWING IN HER PLACE!
TODAY WE DEDICATE THE ROYAL BANK OF SAINT MARTIN...
...OUR NEW VAULT IS FIVE INCHES THICK, NO MAN COULD EVER ROB IT!

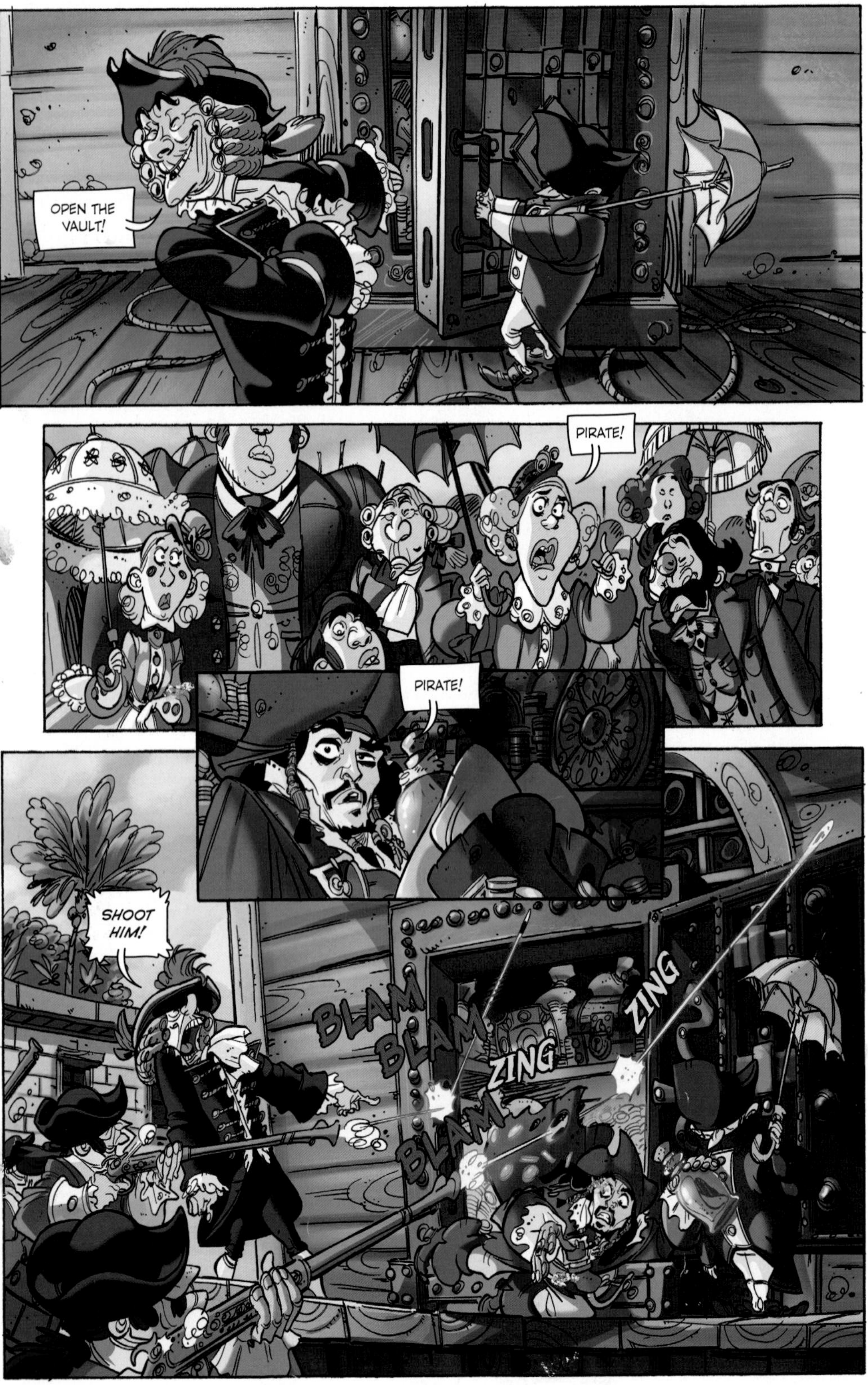

OPEN THE VAULT!
PIRATE!
PIRATE!
SHOOT HIM!
BLAM
BLAM
ZING
BLAM
ZING

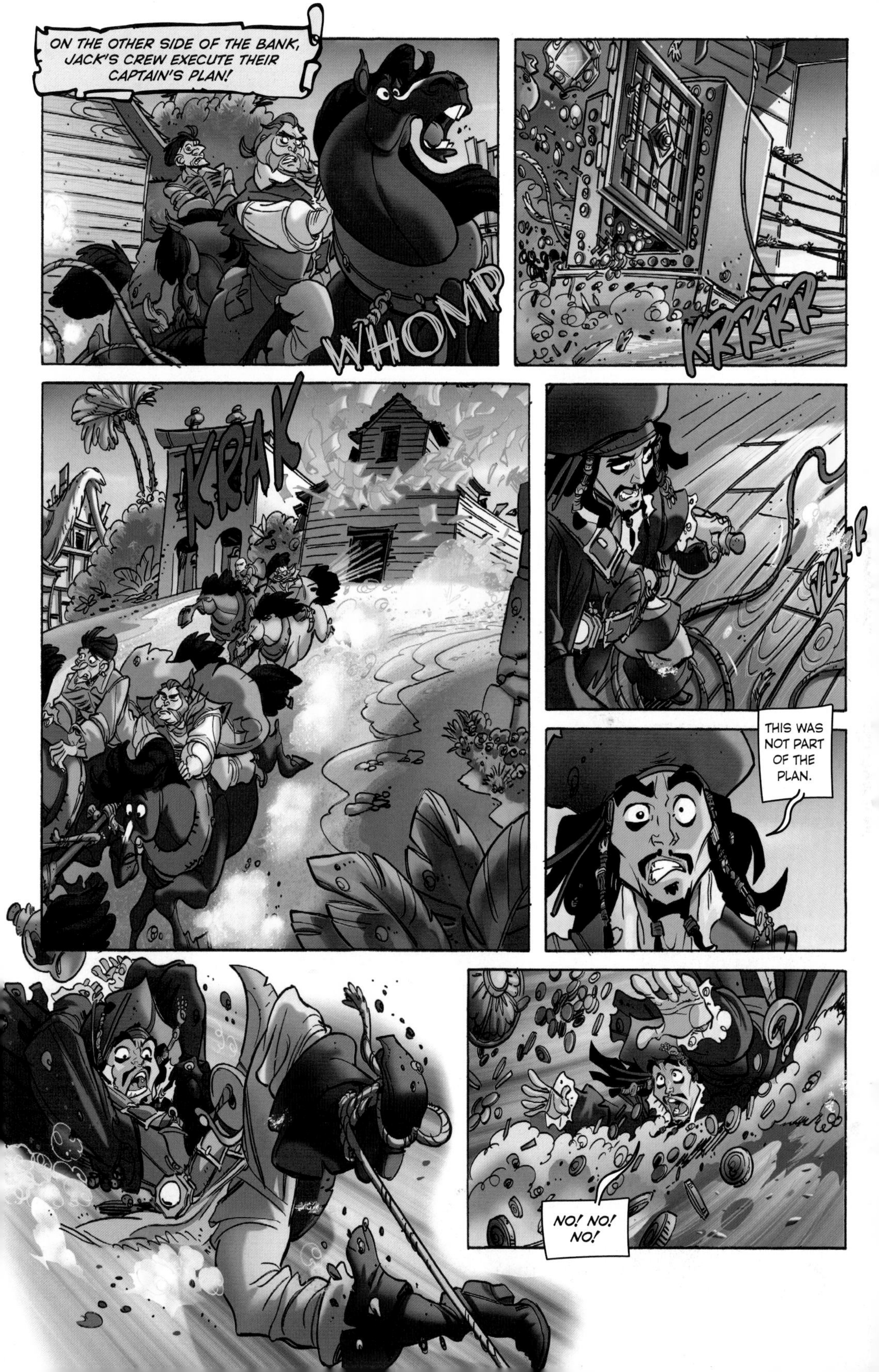
ON THE OTHER SIDE OF THE BANK, JACK'S CREW EXECUTE THEIR CAPTAIN'S PLAN!
WHOMP
KRRRR
KRAK
VRRRR
THIS WAS NOT PART OF THE PLAN.
NO! NO! NO!

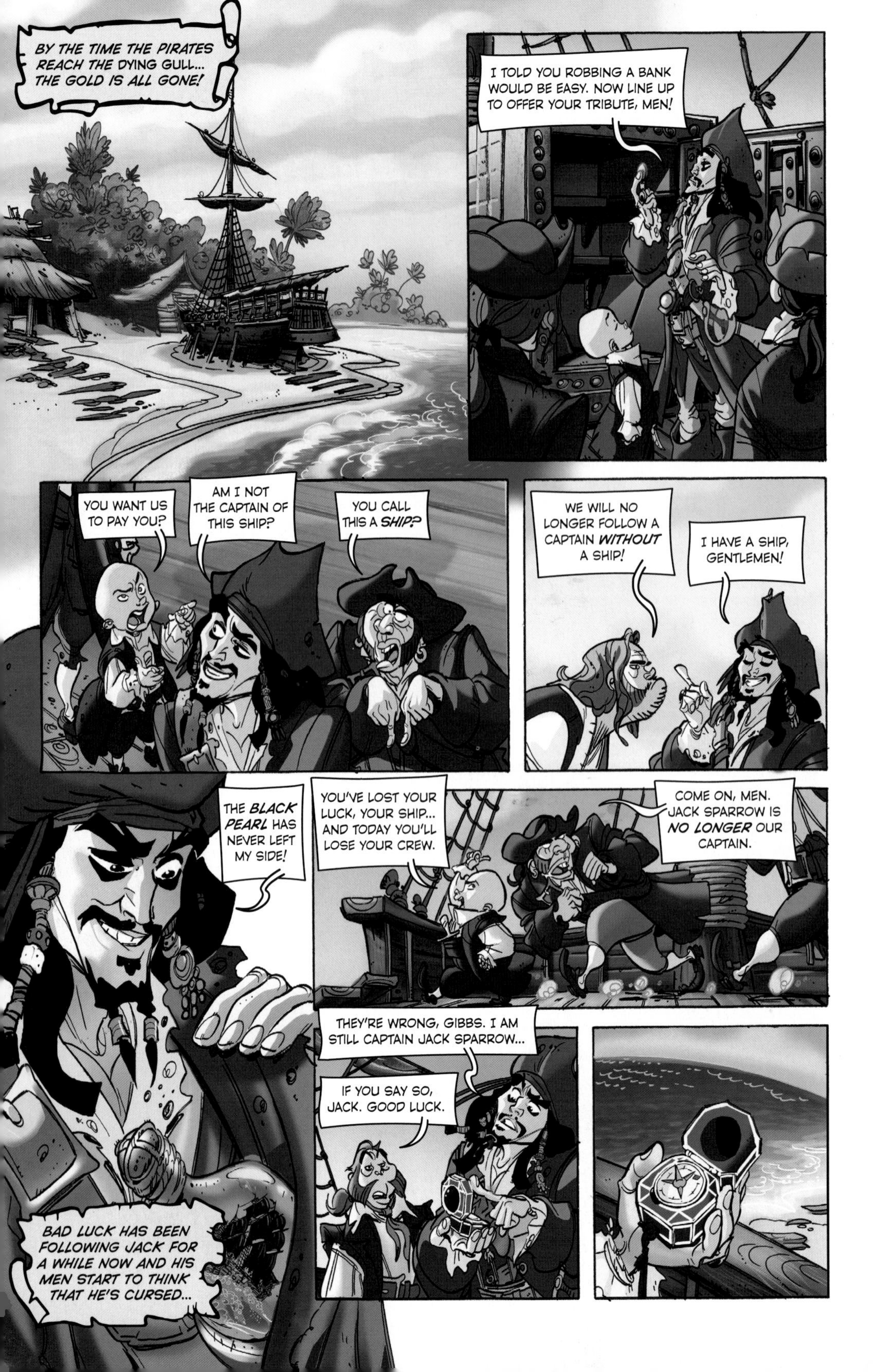
BY THE TIME THE PIRATES REACH THE DYING GULL... THE GOLD IS ALL GONE!
I TOLD YOU ROBBING A BANK WOULD BE EASY. NOW LINE UP TO OFFER YOUR TRIBUTE, MEN!
YOU WANT US TO PAY YOU?
AM I NOT THE CAPTAIN OF THIS SHIP?
YOU CALL THIS A SHIP?
WE WILL NO LONGER FOLLOW A CAPTAIN WITHOUT A SHIP!
I HAVE A SHIP, GENTLEMEN!
THE BLACK PEARL HAS NEVER LEFT MY SIDE!
YOU'VE LOST YOUR LUCK, YOUR SHIP... AND TODAY YOU'LL LOSE YOUR CREW.
COME ON, MEN. JACK SPARROW IS NO LONGER OUR CAPTAIN.
BAD LUCK HAS BEEN FOLLOWING JACK FOR A WHILE NOW AND HIS MEN START TO THINK THAT HE'S CURSED...
THEY'RE WRONG, GIBBS. I AM STILL CAPTAIN JACK SPARROW...
IF YOU SAY SO, JACK. GOOD LUCK.

Everyone in town speaks of him,
the only survivor of the **Monarch** who jabbers about the Trident of Poseidon.
Henry Turner wakes up in a military hospital, his hands shackled to the bed. Lieutenant Scarfield
knows he is a traitor, and is going to execute him. But there's someone else who heard about him,
someone who is looking for the same treasure he seeks: Carina Smyth, who enters the hospital dressed
as a nun. She does not believe in curses, she believes in modern science: to find the Trident
would mean to solve the Map No Man Can Read, a map hidden in the stars...

THIS IS THE *DIARY OF GALILEO GALILEI.* HE SPENT HIS LIFE LOOKING FOR THE MAP. THIS IS WHY HE INVENTED THE SPYGLASS...

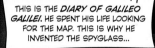

THIS DIARY WAS LEFT ME BY MY *FATHER,* WHOM I NEVER MET. HE BELIEVED I COULD FIND WHAT NO MAN HAS EVER FOUND AND I WILL NOT LET HIM DOWN.

SOON THERE WILL BE A *BLOOD MOON.* ONLY THEN WILL THE MAP BE READ...AND THE TRIDENT FOUND!

CARINA SMYTH!

!

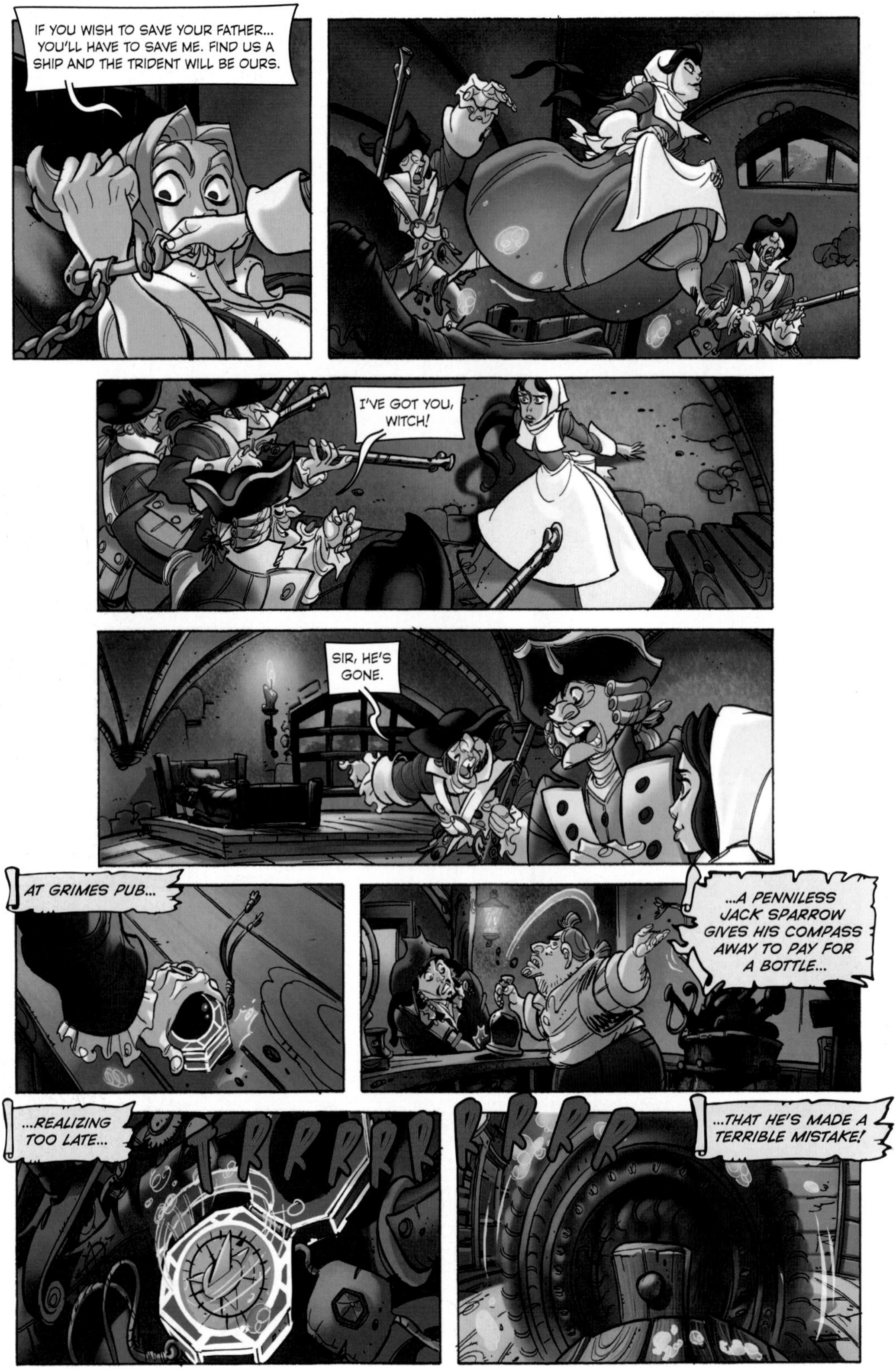
IF YOU WISH TO SAVE YOUR FATHER... YOU'LL HAVE TO SAVE ME. FIND US A SHIP AND THE TRIDENT WILL BE OURS.
I'VE GOT YOU, WITCH!
SIR, HE'S GONE.
AT GRIMES PUB...
...A PENNILESS JACK SPARROW GIVES HIS COMPASS AWAY TO PAY FOR A BOTTLE...
...REALIZING TOO LATE...
TRRRRRRRRRRR
...THAT HE'S MADE A TERRIBLE MISTAKE!

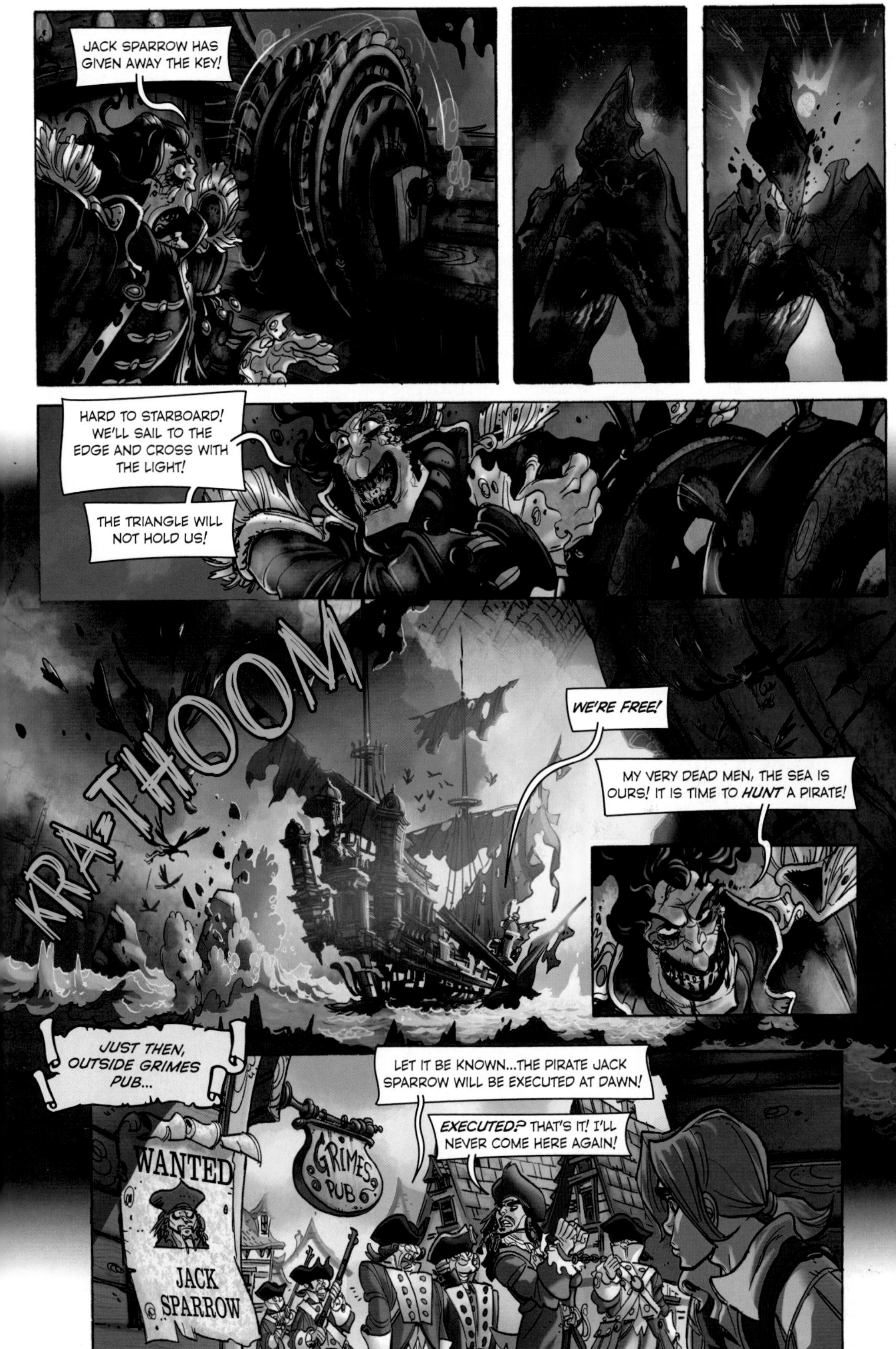

JACK SPARROW HAS GIVEN AWAY THE KEY!
HARD TO STARBOARD! WE'LL SAIL TO THE EDGE AND CROSS WITH THE LIGHT!
THE TRIANGLE WILL NOT HOLD US!
KRA-THOOM
WE'RE FREE!
MY VERY DEAD MEN, THE SEA IS OURS! IT IS TIME TO HUNT A PIRATE!
JUST THEN, OUTSIDE GRIMES PUB...
LET IT BE KNOWN...THE PIRATE JACK SPARROW WILL BE EXECUTED AT DAWN!
EXECUTED?! THAT'S IT! I'LL NEVER COME HERE AGAIN!
GRIMES PUB
WANTED
JACK SPARROW

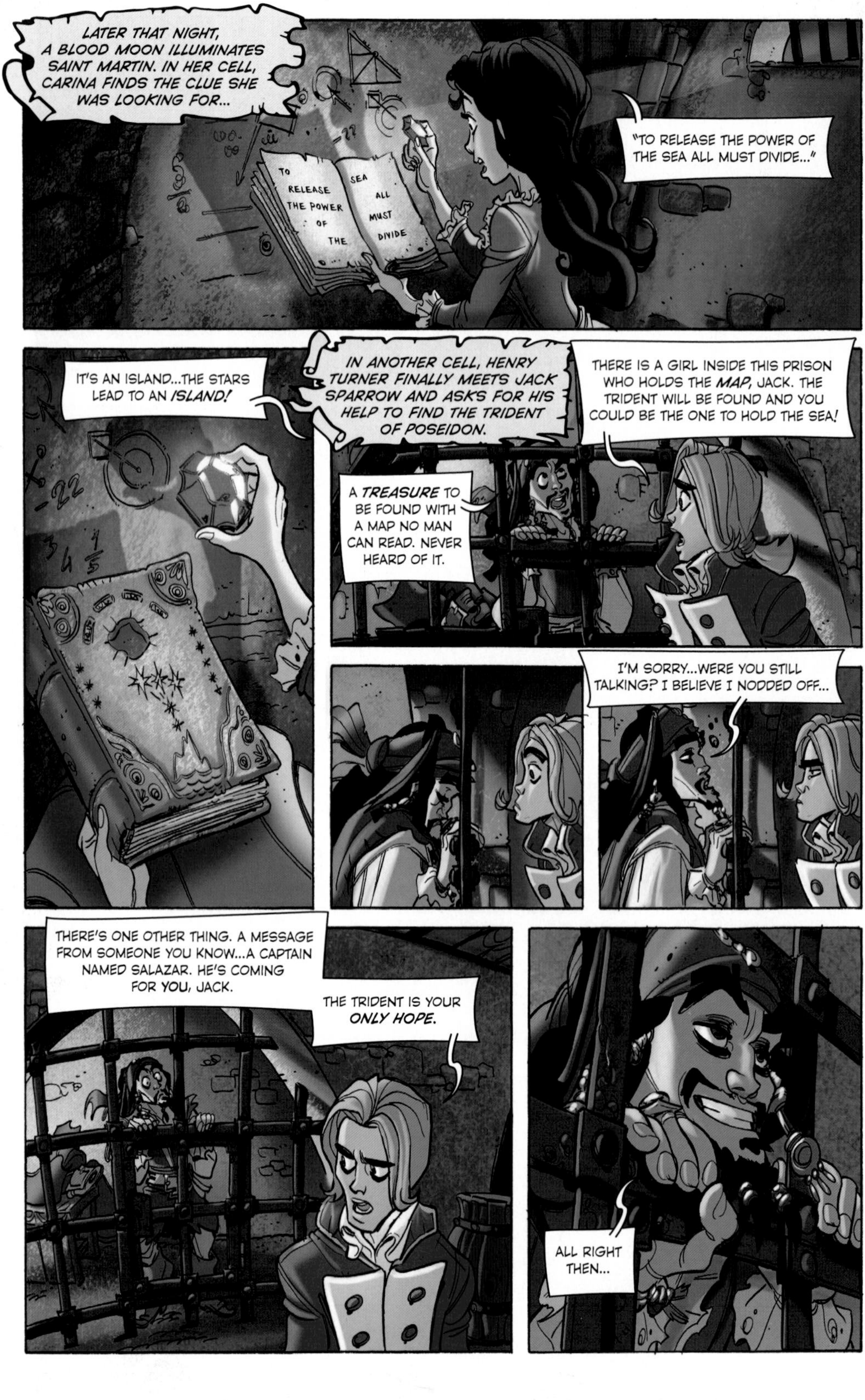
LATER THAT NIGHT, A BLOOD MOON ILLUMINATES SAINT MARTIN. IN HER CELL, CARINA FINDS THE CLUE SHE WAS LOOKING FOR...
"TO RELEASE THE POWER OF THE SEA ALL MUST DIVIDE..."
TO RELEASE THE POWER OF THE SEA ALL MUST DIVIDE
IT'S AN ISLAND...THE STARS LEAD TO AN *ISLAND!*
IN ANOTHER CELL, HENRY TURNER FINALLY MEETS JACK SPARROW AND ASKS FOR HIS HELP TO FIND THE TRIDENT OF POSEIDON.
THERE IS A GIRL INSIDE THIS PRISON WHO HOLDS THE *MAP*, JACK. THE TRIDENT WILL BE FOUND AND YOU COULD BE THE ONE TO HOLD THE SEA!
A *TREASURE* TO BE FOUND WITH A MAP NO MAN CAN READ. NEVER HEARD OF IT.
I'M SORRY...WERE YOU STILL TALKING? I BELIEVE I NODDED OFF...
THERE'S ONE OTHER THING. A MESSAGE FROM SOMEONE YOU KNOW...A CAPTAIN NAMED SALAZAR. HE'S COMING FOR **YOU**, JACK.
THE TRIDENT IS YOUR *ONLY HOPE.*
ALL RIGHT THEN...

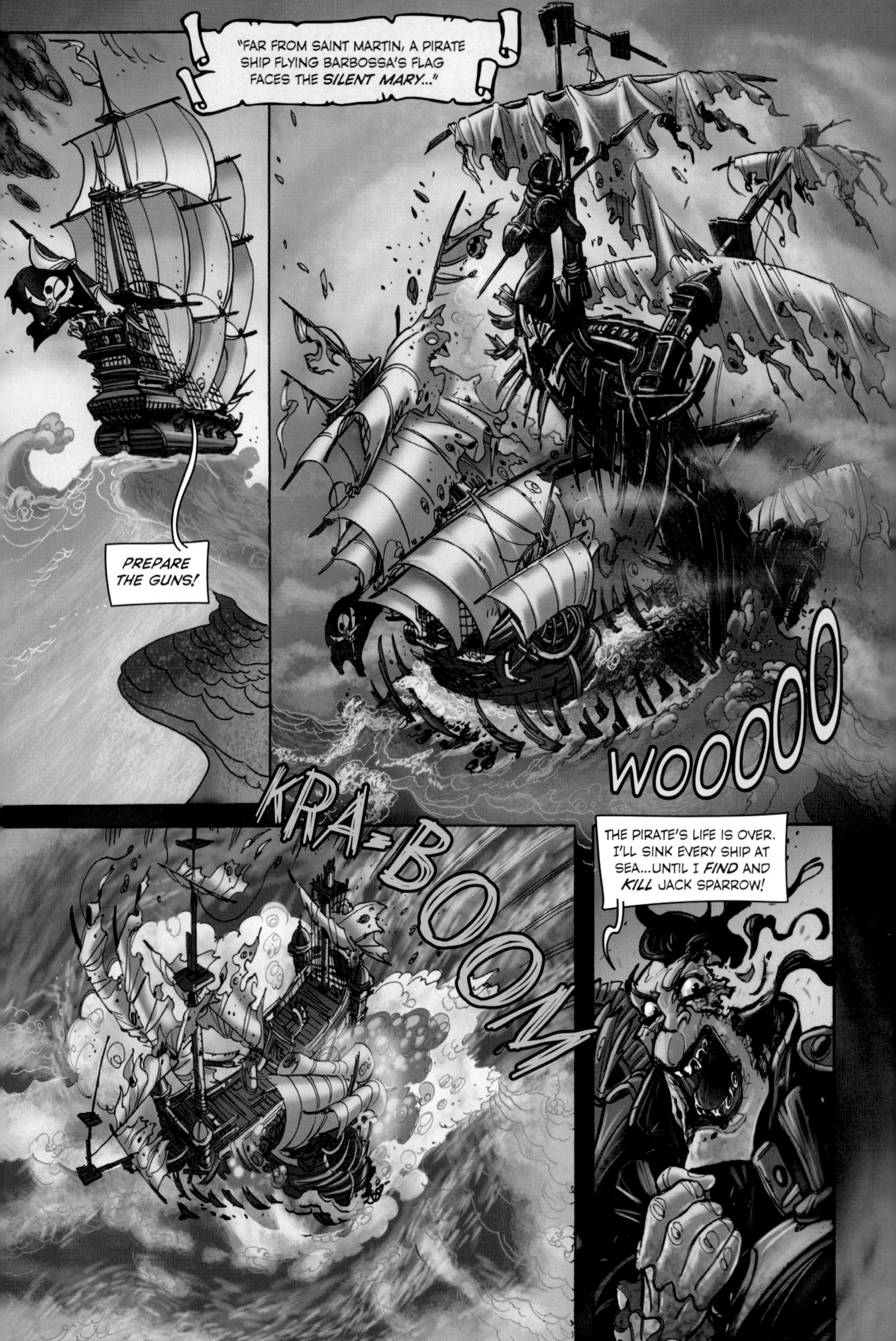
"FAR FROM SAINT MARTIN, A PIRATE SHIP FLYING BARBOSSA'S FLAG FACES THE *SILENT MARY*..."
PREPARE THE GUNS!
WOOOOOO
KRA-BOOOM
THE PIRATE'S LIFE IS OVER. I'LL SINK EVERY SHIP AT SEA...UNTIL I *FIND* AND *KILL* JACK SPARROW!

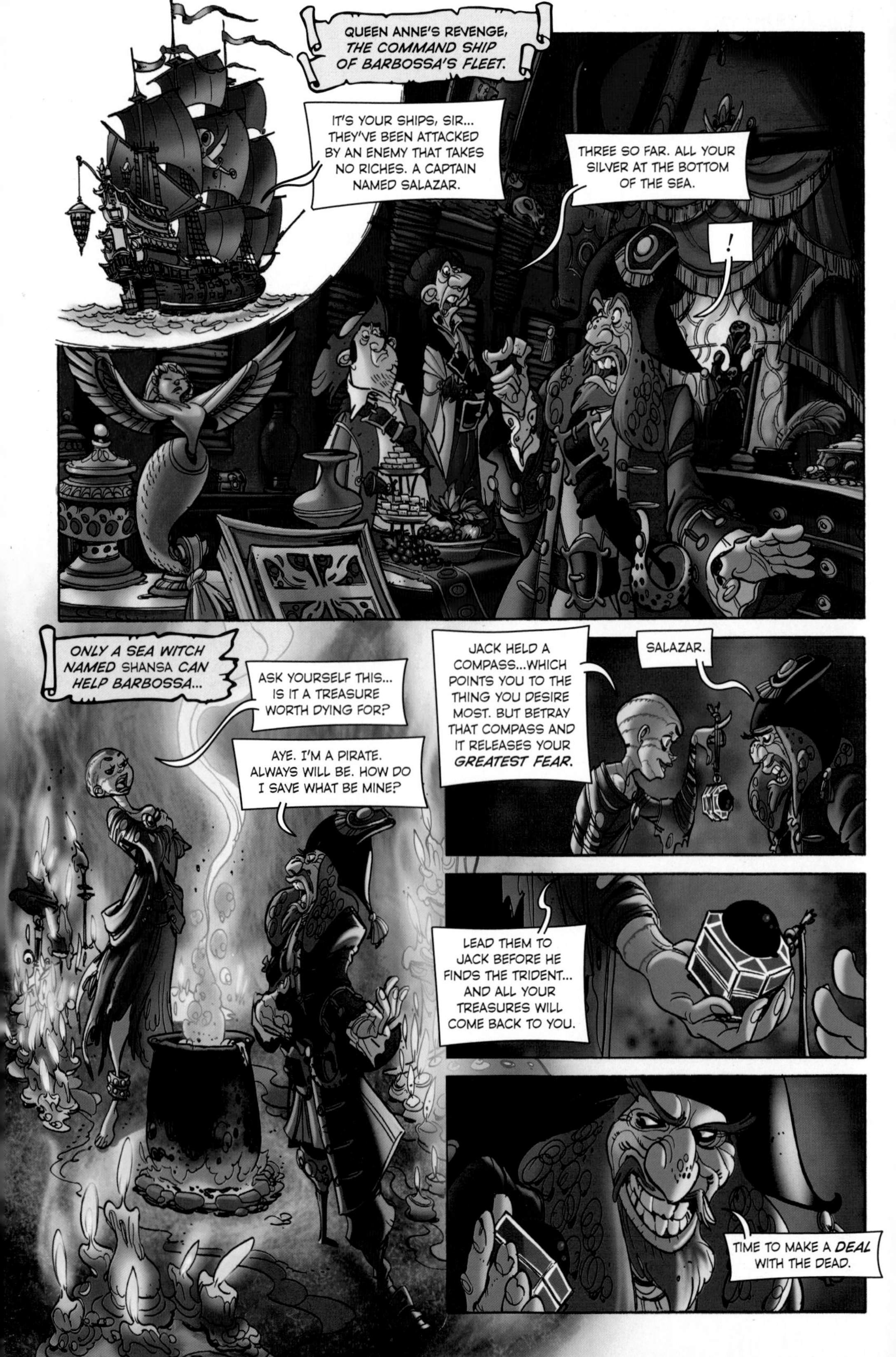
QUEEN ANNE'S REVENGE, THE COMMAND SHIP OF BARBOSSA'S FLEET.
IT'S YOUR SHIPS, SIR... THEY'VE BEEN ATTACKED BY AN ENEMY THAT TAKES NO RICHES. A CAPTAIN NAMED SALAZAR.
THREE SO FAR. ALL YOUR SILVER AT THE BOTTOM OF THE SEA.
!
ONLY A SEA WITCH NAMED SHANSA CAN HELP BARBOSSA...
ASK YOURSELF THIS... IS IT A TREASURE WORTH DYING FOR?
AYE. I'M A PIRATE. ALWAYS WILL BE. HOW DO I SAVE WHAT BE MINE?
JACK HELD A COMPASS...WHICH POINTS YOU TO THE THING YOU DESIRE MOST. BUT BETRAY THAT COMPASS AND IT RELEASES YOUR GREATEST FEAR.
SALAZAR.
LEAD THEM TO JACK BEFORE HE FINDS THE TRIDENT... AND ALL YOUR TREASURES WILL COME BACK TO YOU.
TIME TO MAKE A DEAL WITH THE DEAD.

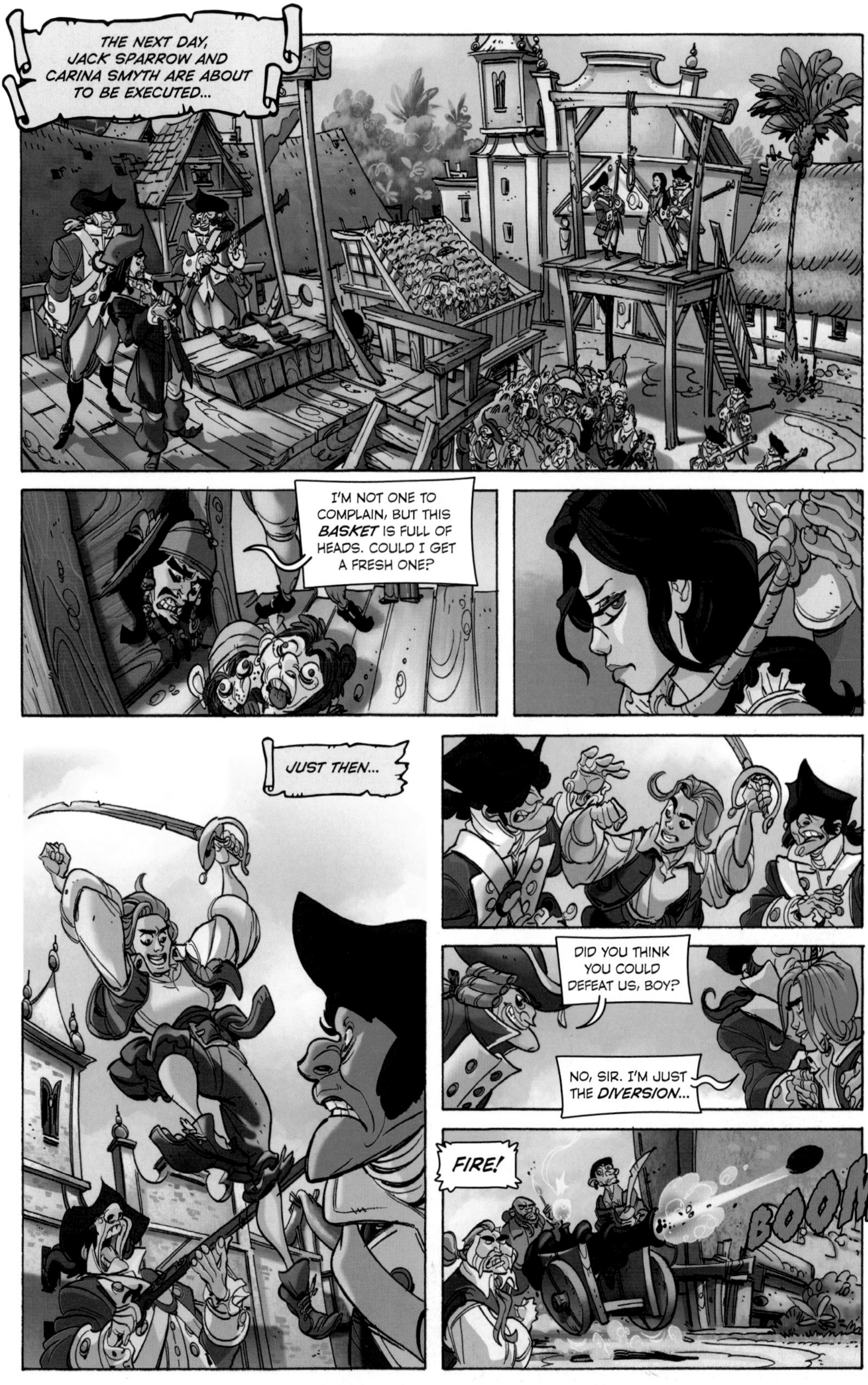
THE NEXT DAY, JACK SPARROW AND CARINA SMYTH ARE ABOUT TO BE EXECUTED...
I'M NOT ONE TO COMPLAIN, BUT THIS BASKET IS FULL OF HEADS. COULD I GET A FRESH ONE?
JUST THEN...
DID YOU THINK YOU COULD DEFEAT US, BOY?
NO, SIR. I'M JUST THE DIVERSION...
FIRE!
BOOM

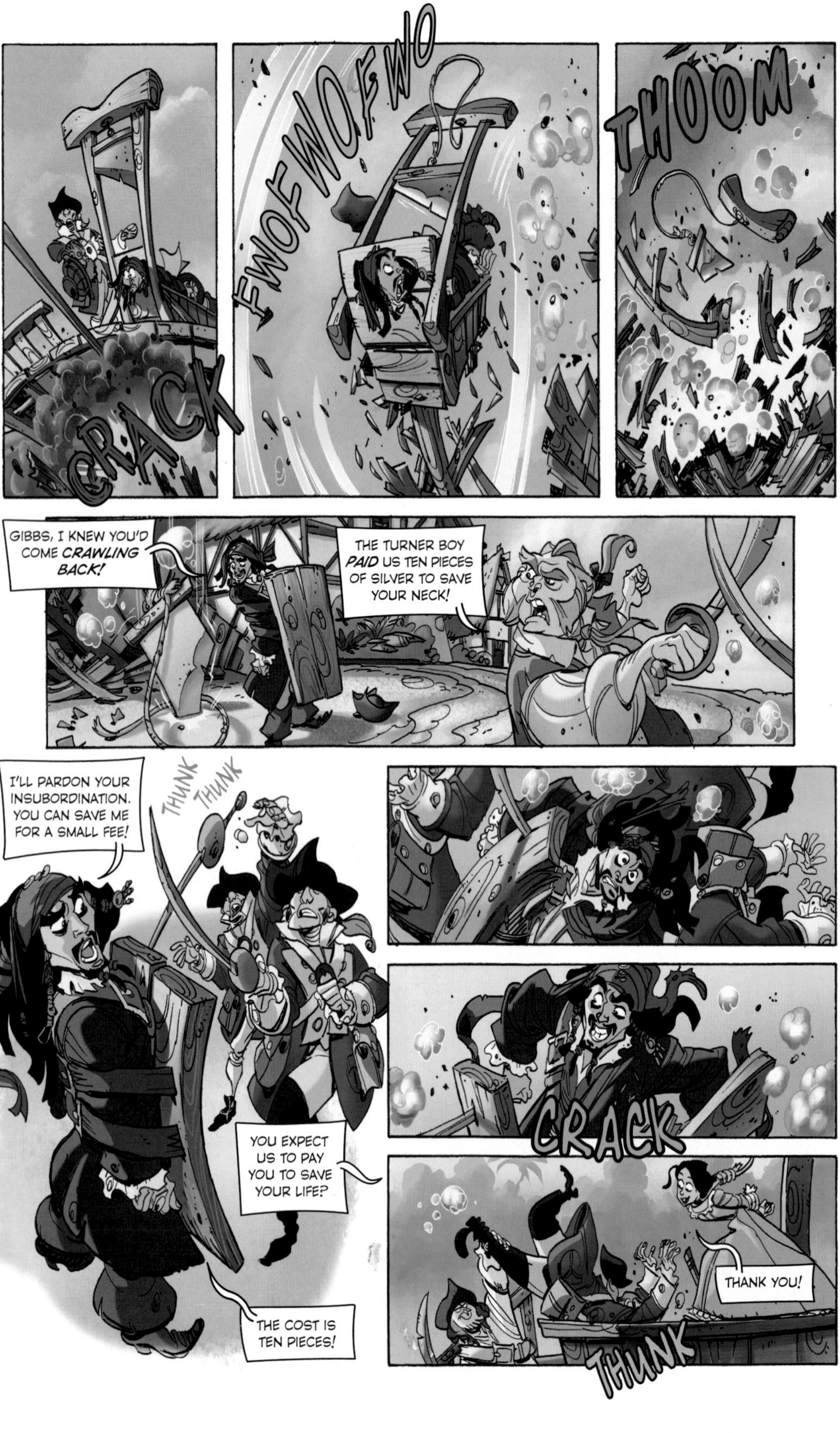
CRACK
FWOFWOFWO
THOOM
GIBBS, I KNEW YOU'D COME *CRAWLING BACK!*
THE TURNER BOY *PAID* US TEN PIECES OF SILVER TO SAVE YOUR NECK!
I'LL PARDON YOUR INSUBORDINATION. YOU CAN SAVE ME FOR A SMALL FEE!
THUNK
THUNK
YOU EXPECT US TO PAY YOU TO SAVE YOUR LIFE?
THE COST IS TEN PIECES!
CRACK
THANK YOU!
THUNK

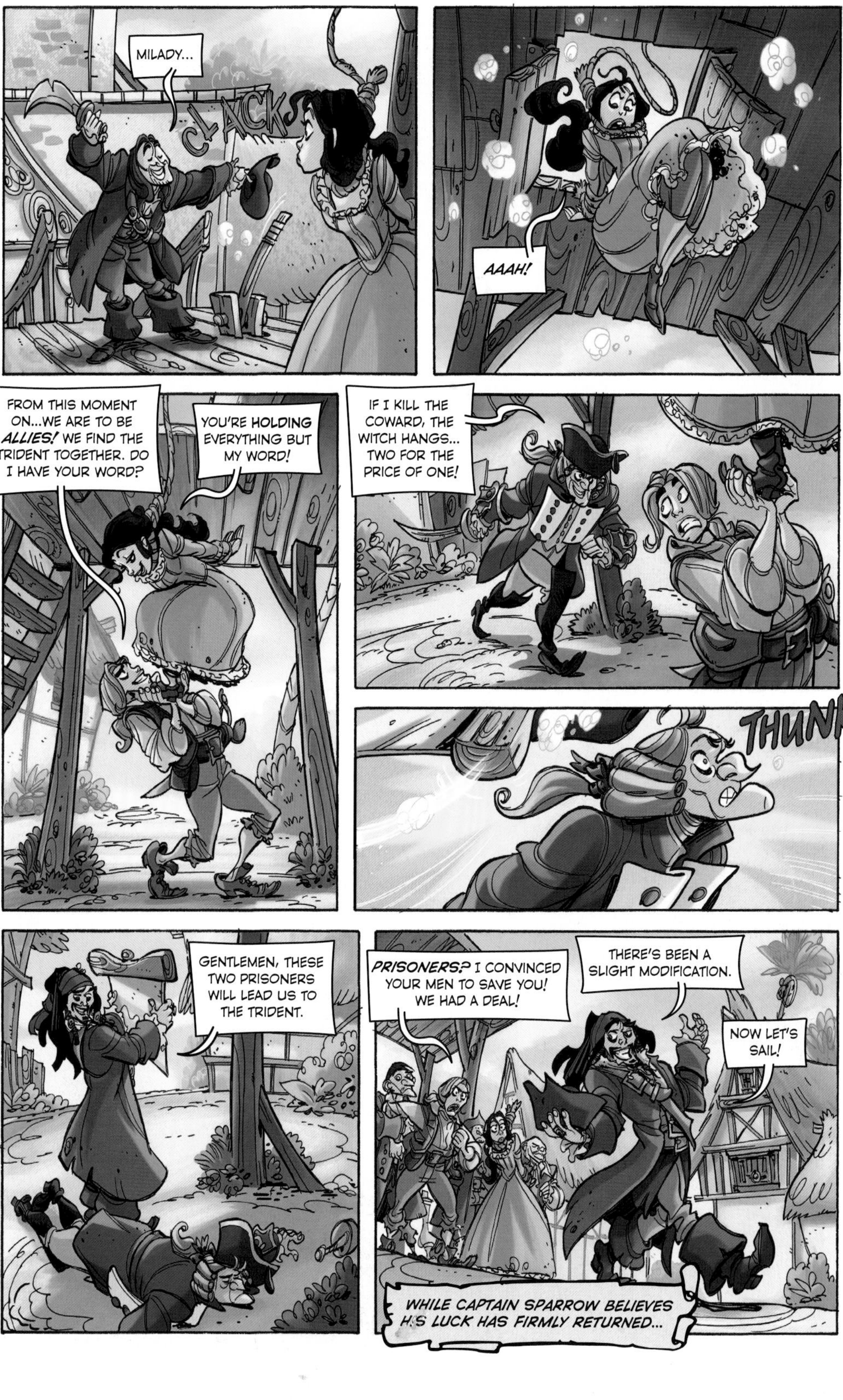
MILADY...
CLACK
AAAH!
FROM THIS MOMENT ON...WE ARE TO BE ALLIES! WE FIND THE TRIDENT TOGETHER. DO I HAVE YOUR WORD?
YOU'RE HOLDING EVERYTHING BUT MY WORD!
IF I KILL THE COWARD, THE WITCH HANGS... TWO FOR THE PRICE OF ONE!
THUNK
GENTLEMEN, THESE TWO PRISONERS WILL LEAD US TO THE TRIDENT.
PRISONERS? I CONVINCED YOUR MEN TO SAVE YOU! WE HAD A DEAL!
THERE'S BEEN A SLIGHT MODIFICATION.
NOW LET'S SAIL!
WHILE CAPTAIN SPARROW BELIEVES HIS LUCK HAS FIRMLY RETURNED...

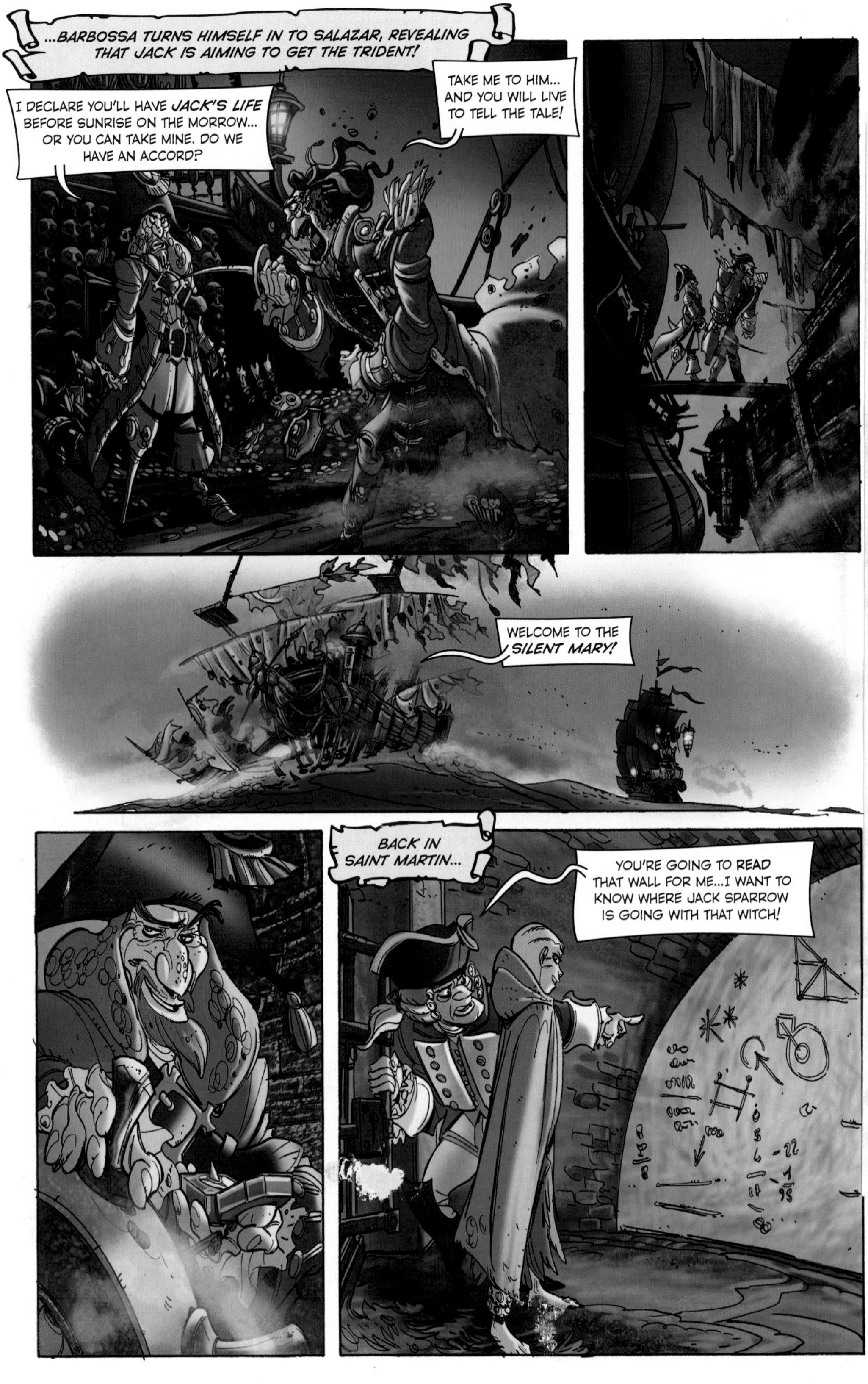

...BARBOSSA TURNS HIMSELF IN TO SALAZAR, REVEALING THAT JACK IS AIMING TO GET THE TRIDENT!
I DECLARE YOU'LL HAVE JACK'S LIFE BEFORE SUNRISE ON THE MORROW... OR YOU CAN TAKE MINE. DO WE HAVE AN ACCORD?
TAKE ME TO HIM... AND YOU WILL LIVE TO TELL THE TALE!
WELCOME TO THE SILENT MARY!
BACK IN SAINT MARTIN...
YOU'RE GOING TO READ THAT WALL FOR ME...I WANT TO KNOW WHERE JACK SPARROW IS GOING WITH THAT WITCH!

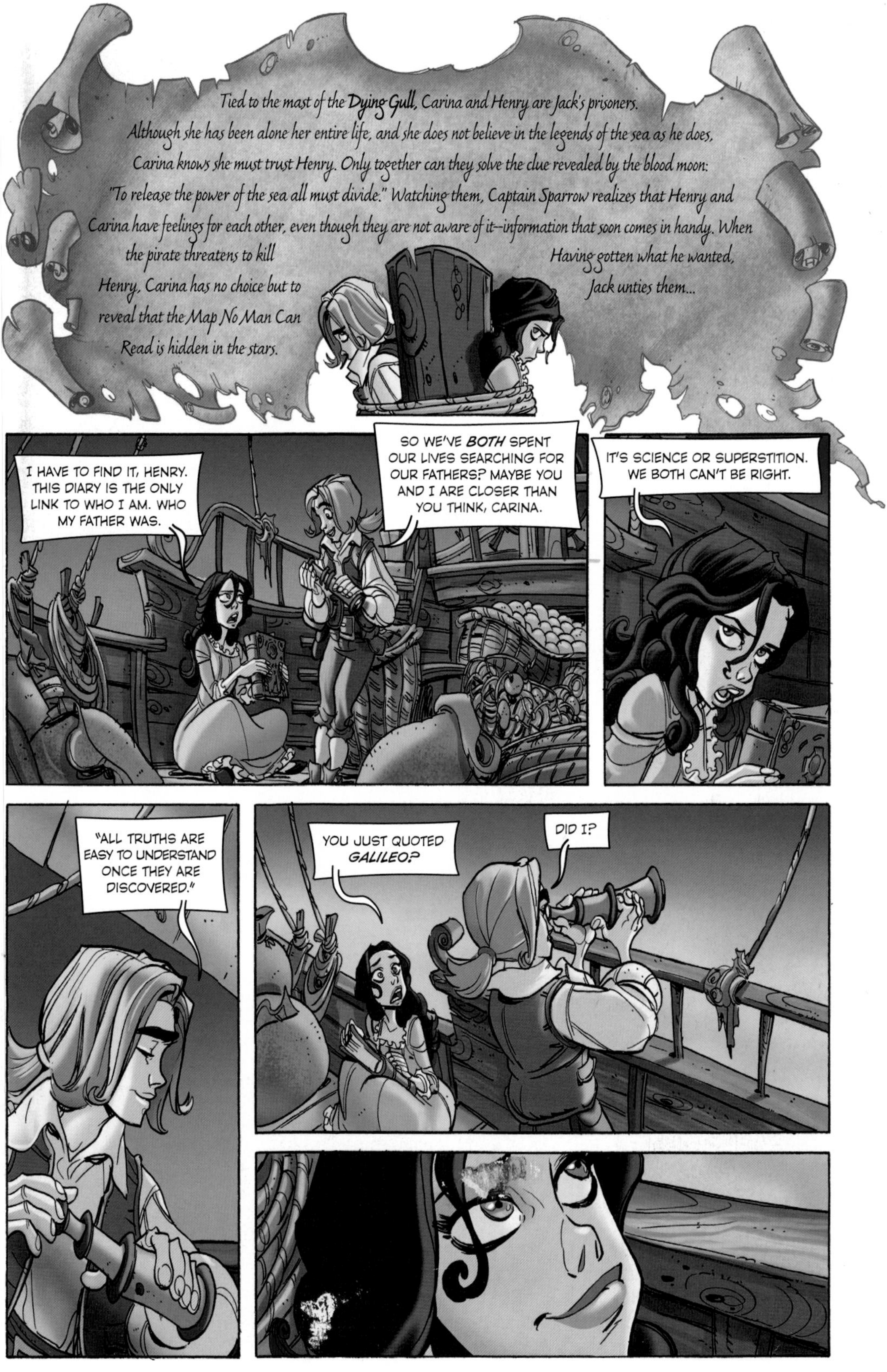

Tied to the mast of the Dying Gull, Carina and Henry are Jack's prisoners. Although she has been alone her entire life, and she does not believe in the legends of the sea as he does, Carina knows she must trust Henry. Only together can they solve the clue revealed by the blood moon: "To release the power of the sea all must divide." Watching them, Captain Sparrow realizes that Henry and Carina have feelings for each other, even though they are not aware of it--information that soon comes in handy. When the pirate threatens to kill Henry, Carina has no choice but to reveal that the Map No Man Can Read is hidden in the stars. Having gotten what he wanted, Jack unties them...
I HAVE TO FIND IT, HENRY. THIS DIARY IS THE ONLY LINK TO WHO I AM. WHO MY FATHER WAS.
SO WE'VE BOTH SPENT OUR LIVES SEARCHING FOR OUR FATHERS? MAYBE YOU AND I ARE CLOSER THAN YOU THINK, CARINA.
IT'S SCIENCE OR SUPERSTITION. WE BOTH CAN'T BE RIGHT.
"ALL TRUTHS ARE EASY TO UNDERSTAND ONCE THEY ARE DISCOVERED."
YOU JUST QUOTED GALILEO?
DID I?

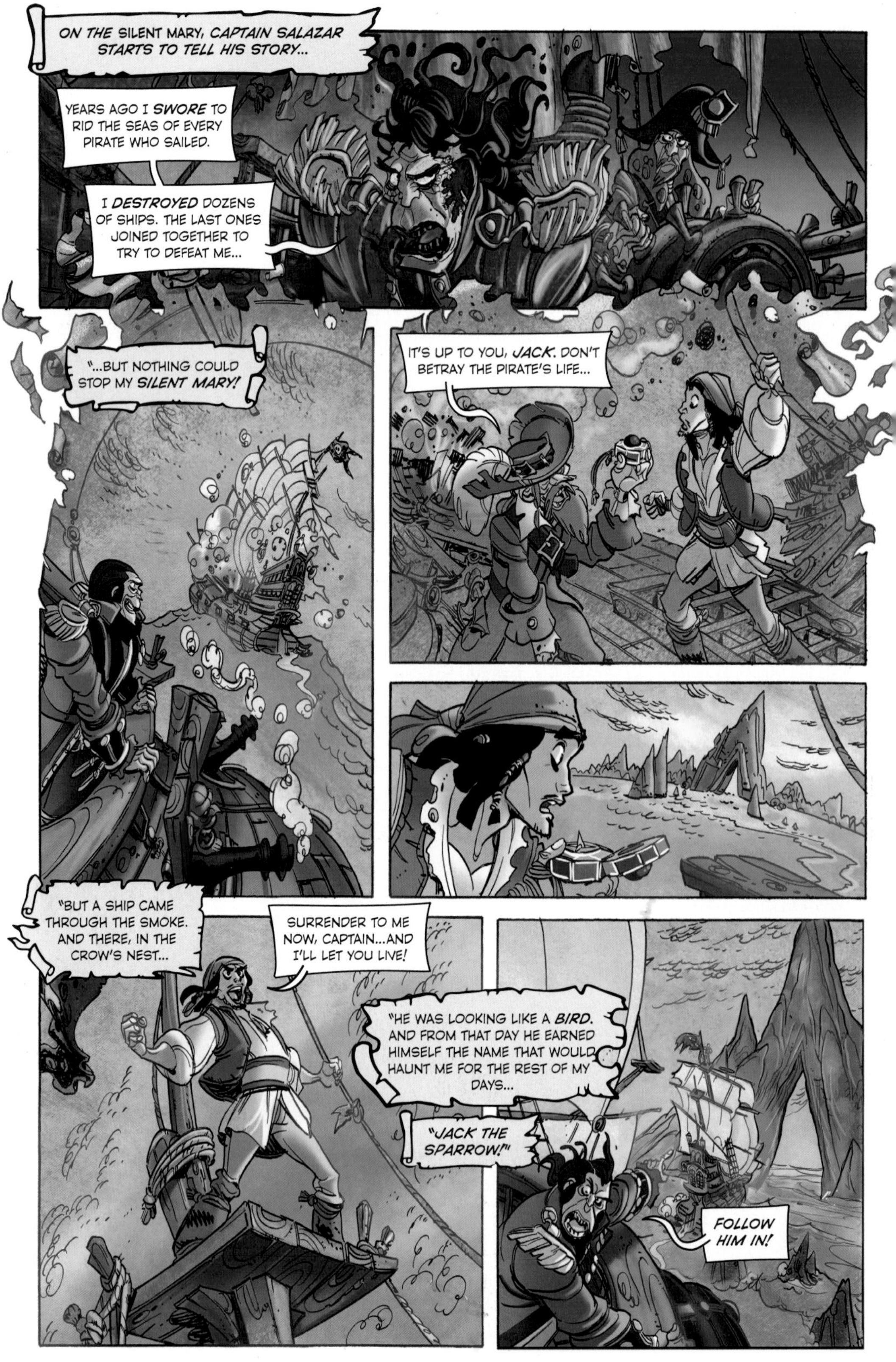
ON THE SILENT MARY, CAPTAIN SALAZAR STARTS TO TELL HIS STORY...
YEARS AGO I SWORE TO RID THE SEAS OF EVERY PIRATE WHO SAILED.
I DESTROYED DOZENS OF SHIPS. THE LAST ONES JOINED TOGETHER TO TRY TO DEFEAT ME...
"...BUT NOTHING COULD STOP MY SILENT MARY!
IT'S UP TO YOU, JACK. DON'T BETRAY THE PIRATE'S LIFE...
"BUT A SHIP CAME THROUGH THE SMOKE. AND THERE, IN THE CROW'S NEST...
SURRENDER TO ME NOW, CAPTAIN...AND I'LL LET YOU LIVE!
"HE WAS LOOKING LIKE A BIRD. AND FROM THAT DAY HE EARNED HIMSELF THE NAME THAT WOULD HAUNT ME FOR THE REST OF MY DAYS...
"JACK THE SPARROW!"
FOLLOW HIM IN!

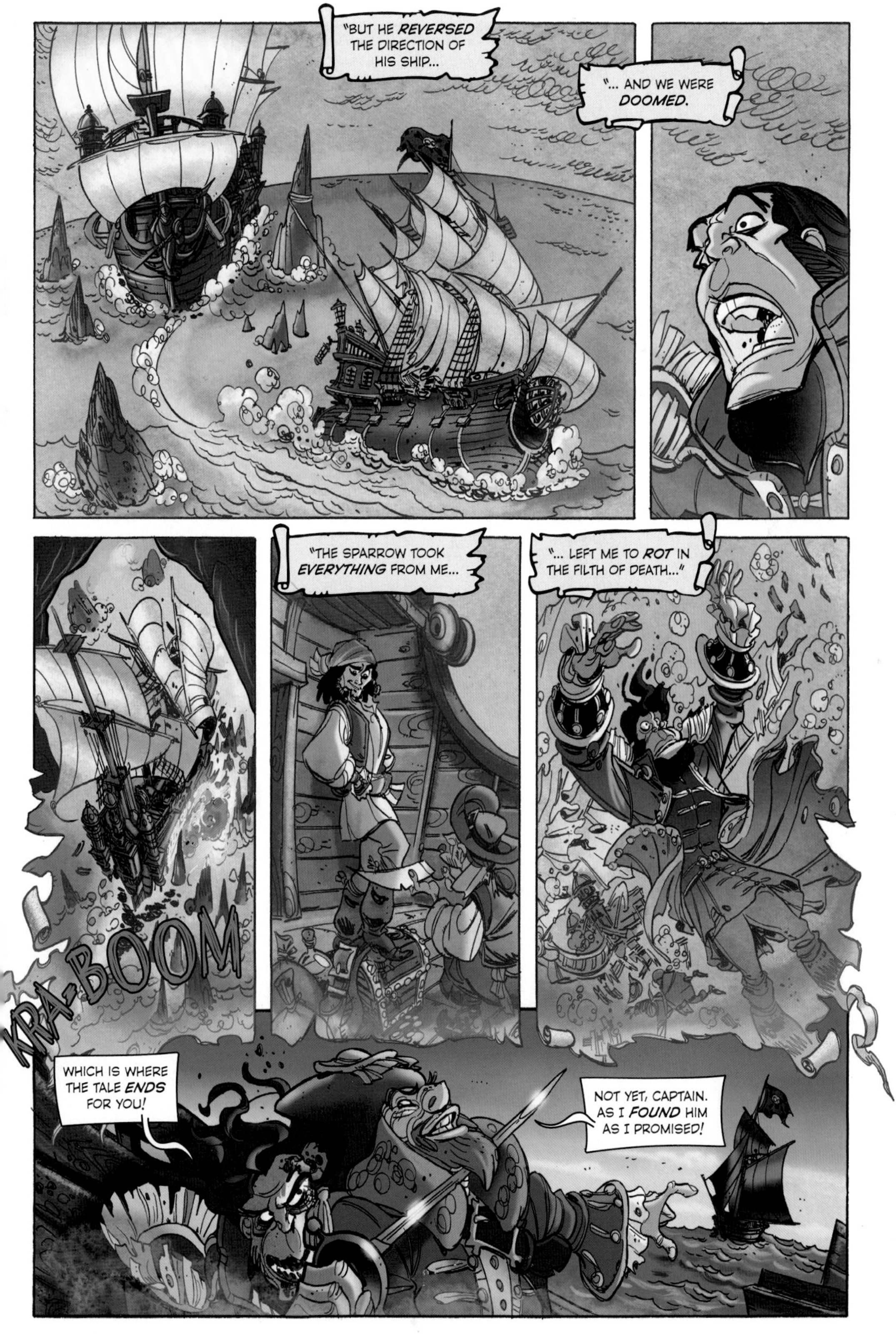
"BUT HE *REVERSED* THE DIRECTION OF HIS SHIP...
"... AND WE WERE ***DOOMED.***
KRA-BOOM
"THE SPARROW TOOK ***EVERYTHING*** FROM ME...
"... LEFT ME TO ***ROT*** IN THE FILTH OF DEATH..."
WHICH IS WHERE THE TALE ***ENDS*** FOR YOU!
NOT YET, CAPTAIN. AS I ***FOUND*** HIM AS I PROMISED!

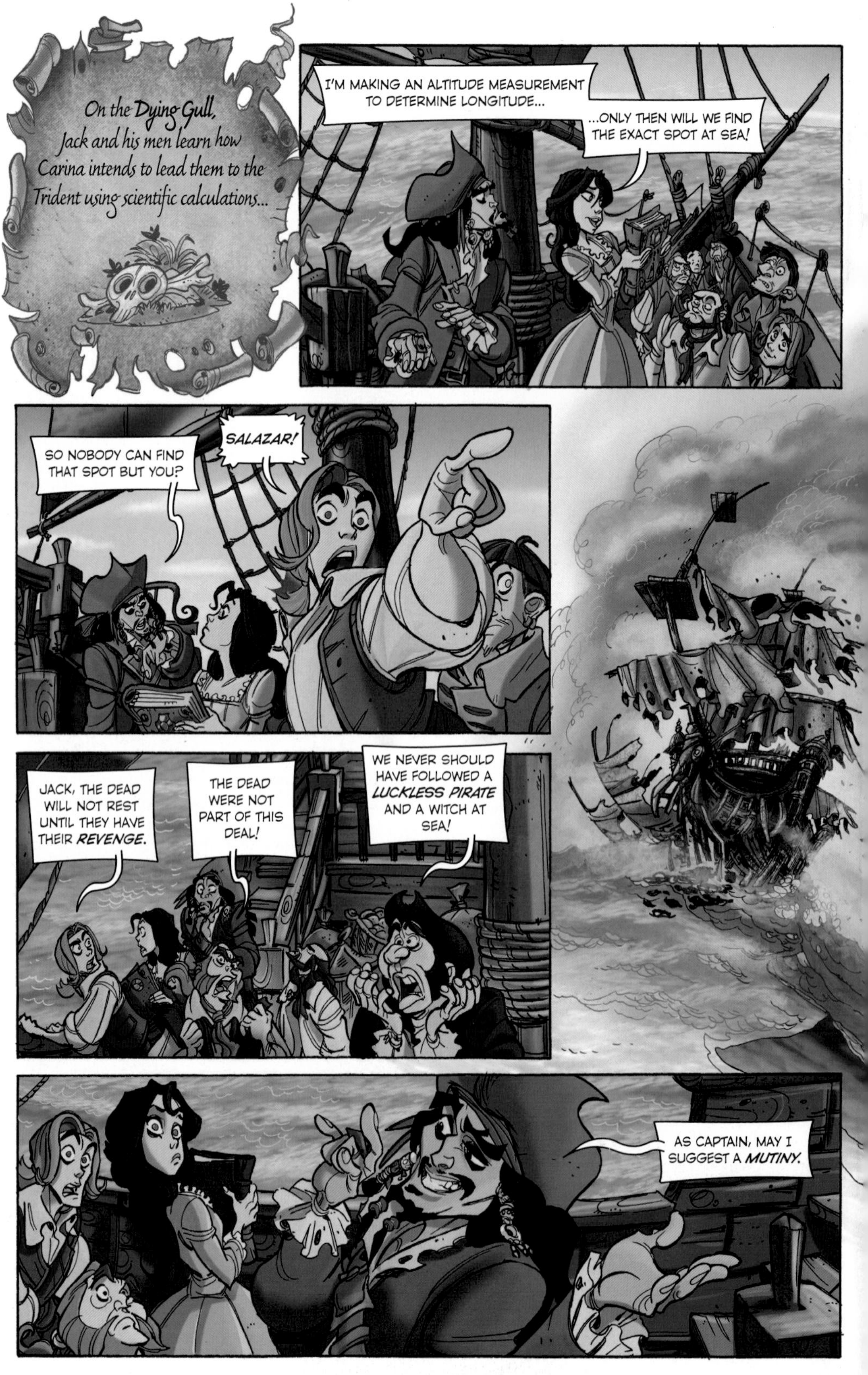

On the Dying Gull, Jack and his men learn how Carina intends to lead them to the Trident using scientific calculations...
I'M MAKING AN ALTITUDE MEASUREMENT TO DETERMINE LONGITUDE...
...ONLY THEN WILL WE FIND THE EXACT SPOT AT SEA!
SO NOBODY CAN FIND THAT SPOT BUT YOU?
SALAZAR!
JACK, THE DEAD WILL NOT REST UNTIL THEY HAVE THEIR REVENGE.
THE DEAD WERE NOT PART OF THIS DEAL!
WE NEVER SHOULD HAVE FOLLOWED A LUCKLESS PIRATE AND A WITCH AT SEA!
AS CAPTAIN, MAY I SUGGEST A MUTINY.

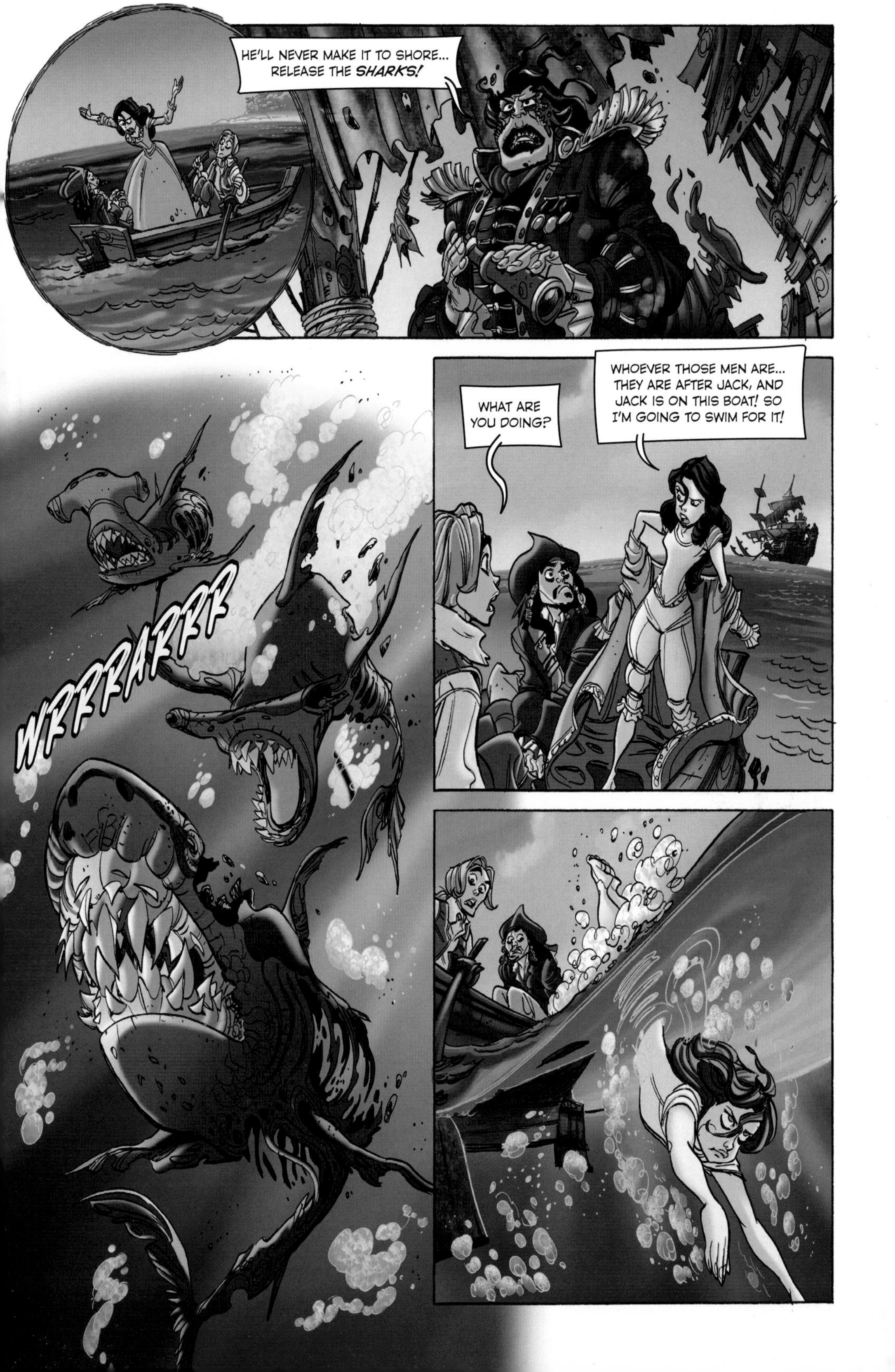
HE'LL NEVER MAKE IT TO SHORE...
RELEASE THE SHARKS!
WRRRARRR
WHAT ARE YOU DOING?
WHOEVER THOSE MEN ARE... THEY ARE AFTER JACK, AND JACK IS ON THIS BOAT! SO I'M GOING TO SWIM FOR IT!

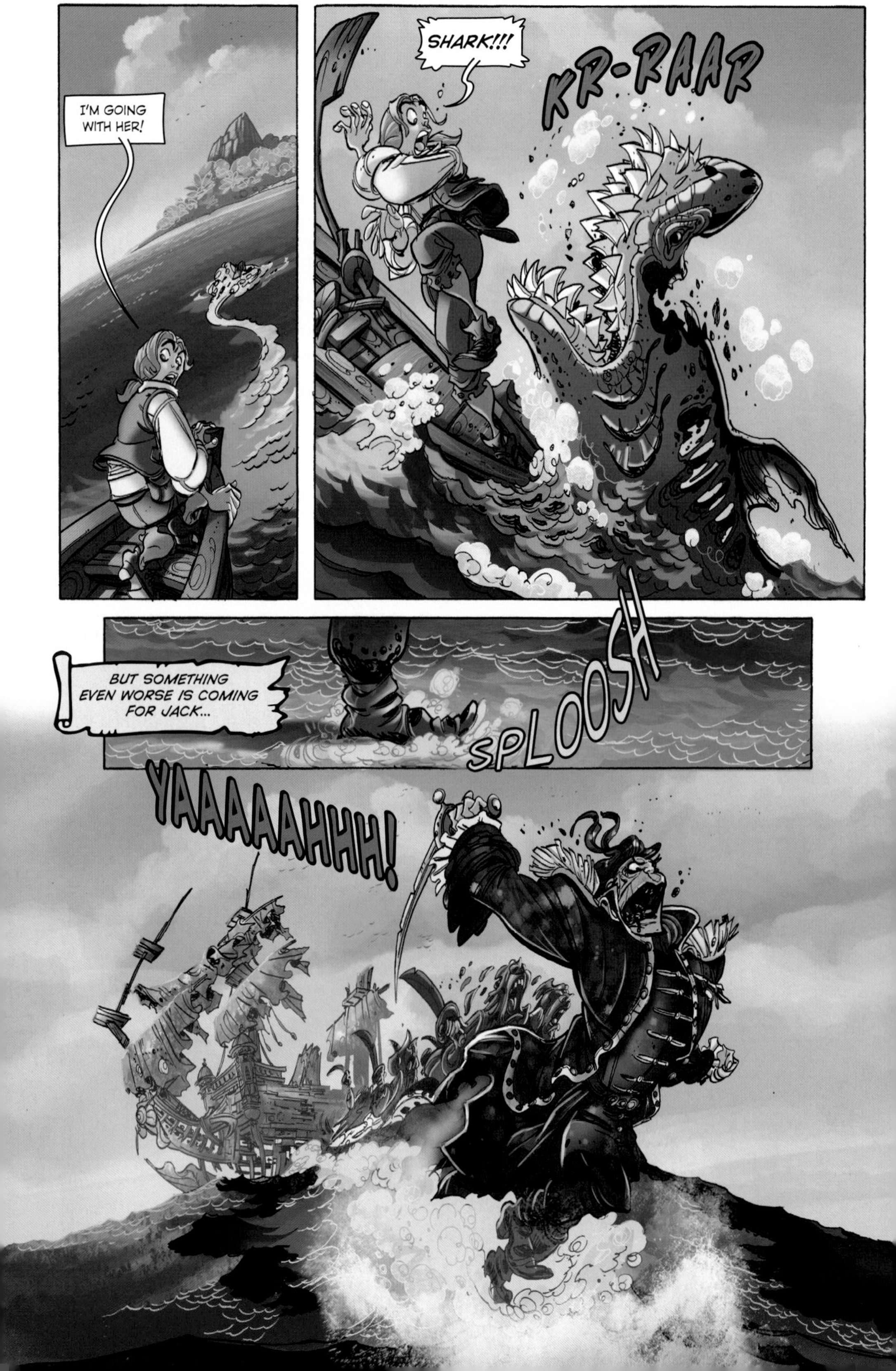
I'M GOING WITH HER!
SHARK!!!
KR-RAAR
BUT SOMETHING EVEN WORSE IS COMING FOR JACK...
SPLOOSH
YAAAAAHHH!

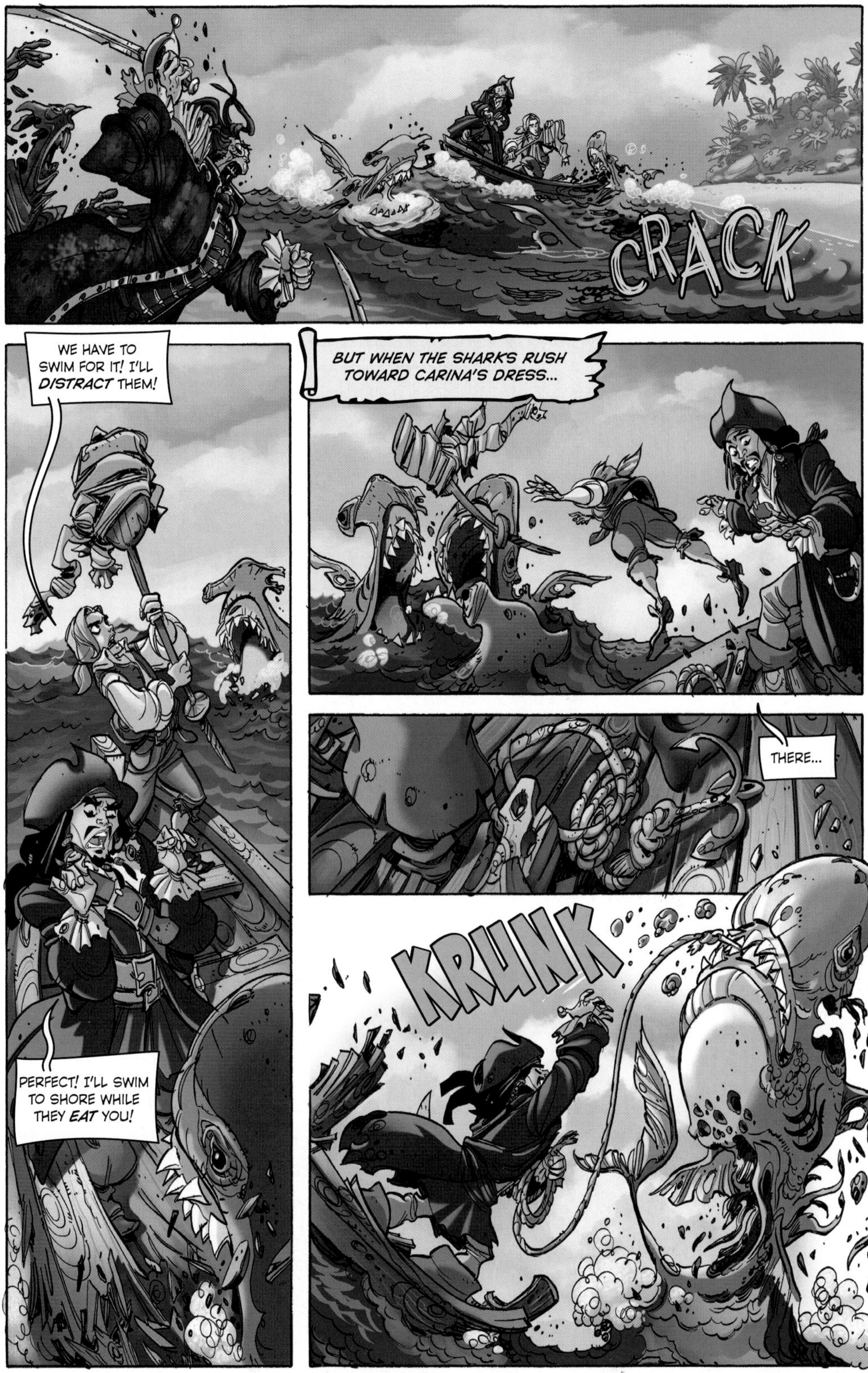
CRACK
WE HAVE TO SWIM FOR IT! I'LL DISTRACT THEM!
PERFECT! I'LL SWIM TO SHORE WHILE THEY EAT YOU!
BUT WHEN THE SHARKS RUSH TOWARD CARINA'S DRESS...
THERE...
KRUNK

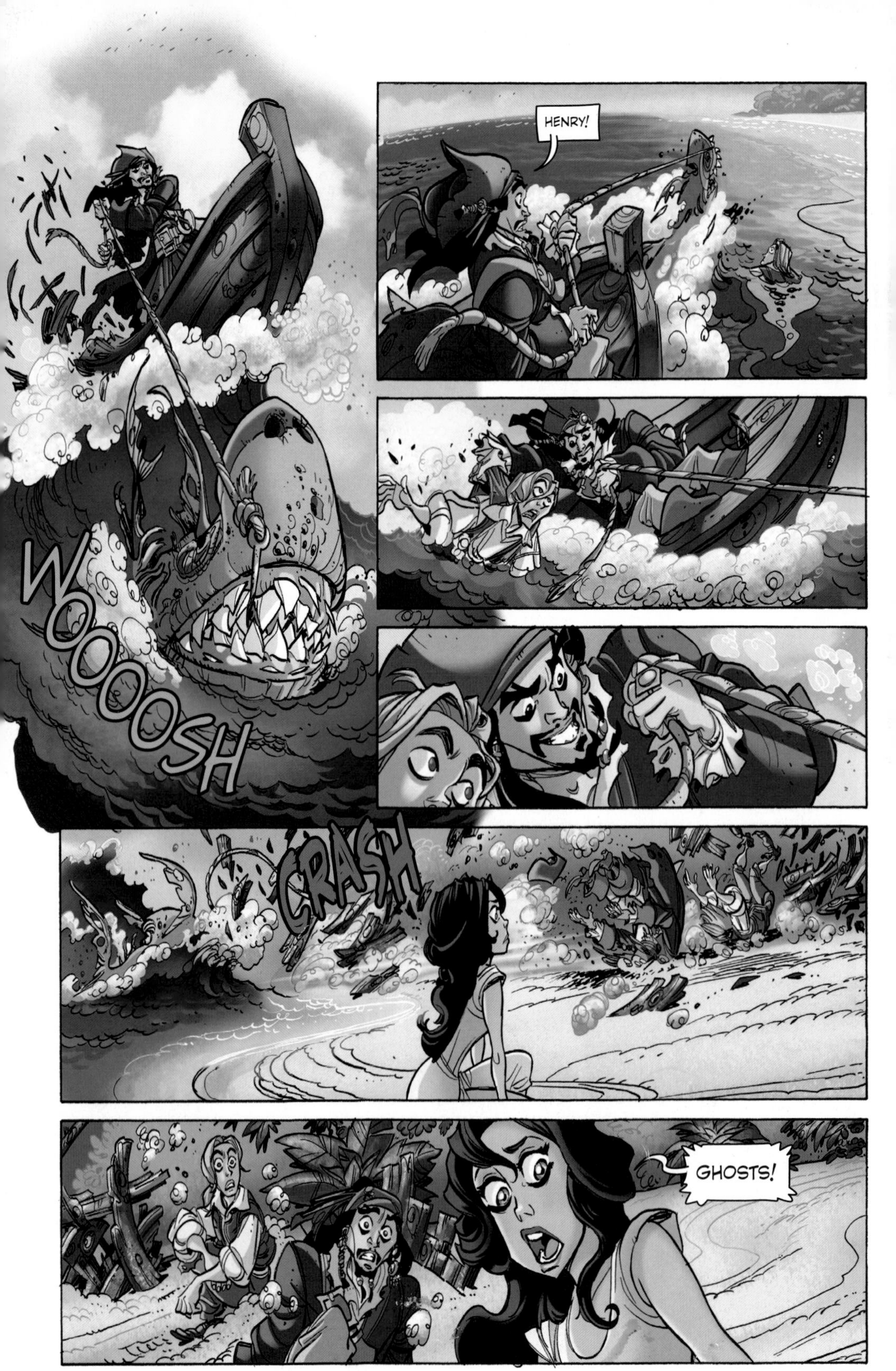

WOOOOOSH
HENRY!
CRASH
GHOSTS!

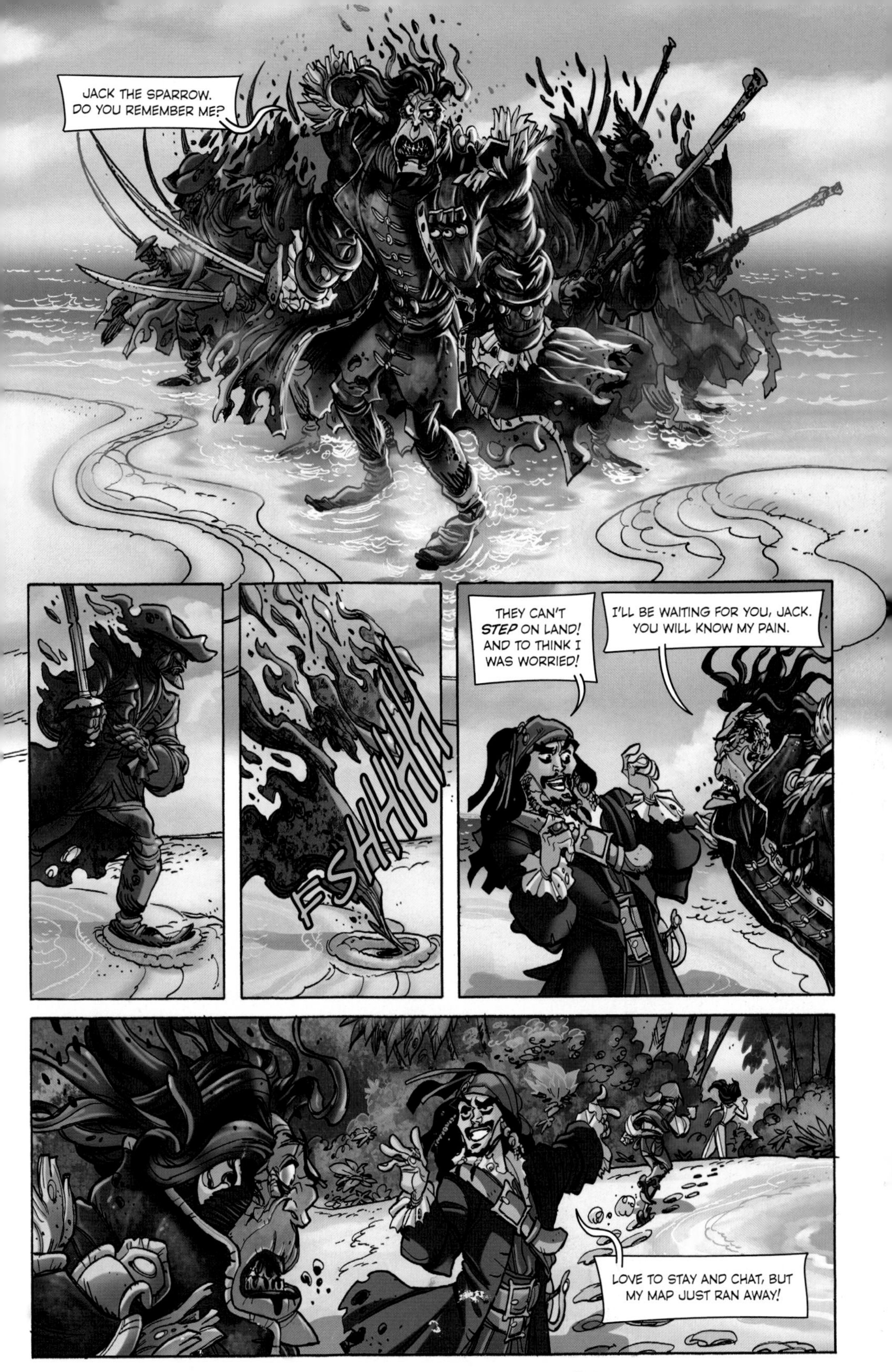
JACK THE SPARROW. DO YOU REMEMBER ME?
FSHHHHH
THEY CAN'T STEP ON LAND! AND TO THINK I WAS WORRIED!
I'LL BE WAITING FOR YOU, JACK. YOU WILL KNOW MY PAIN.
LOVE TO STAY AND CHAT, BUT MY MAP JUST RAN AWAY!

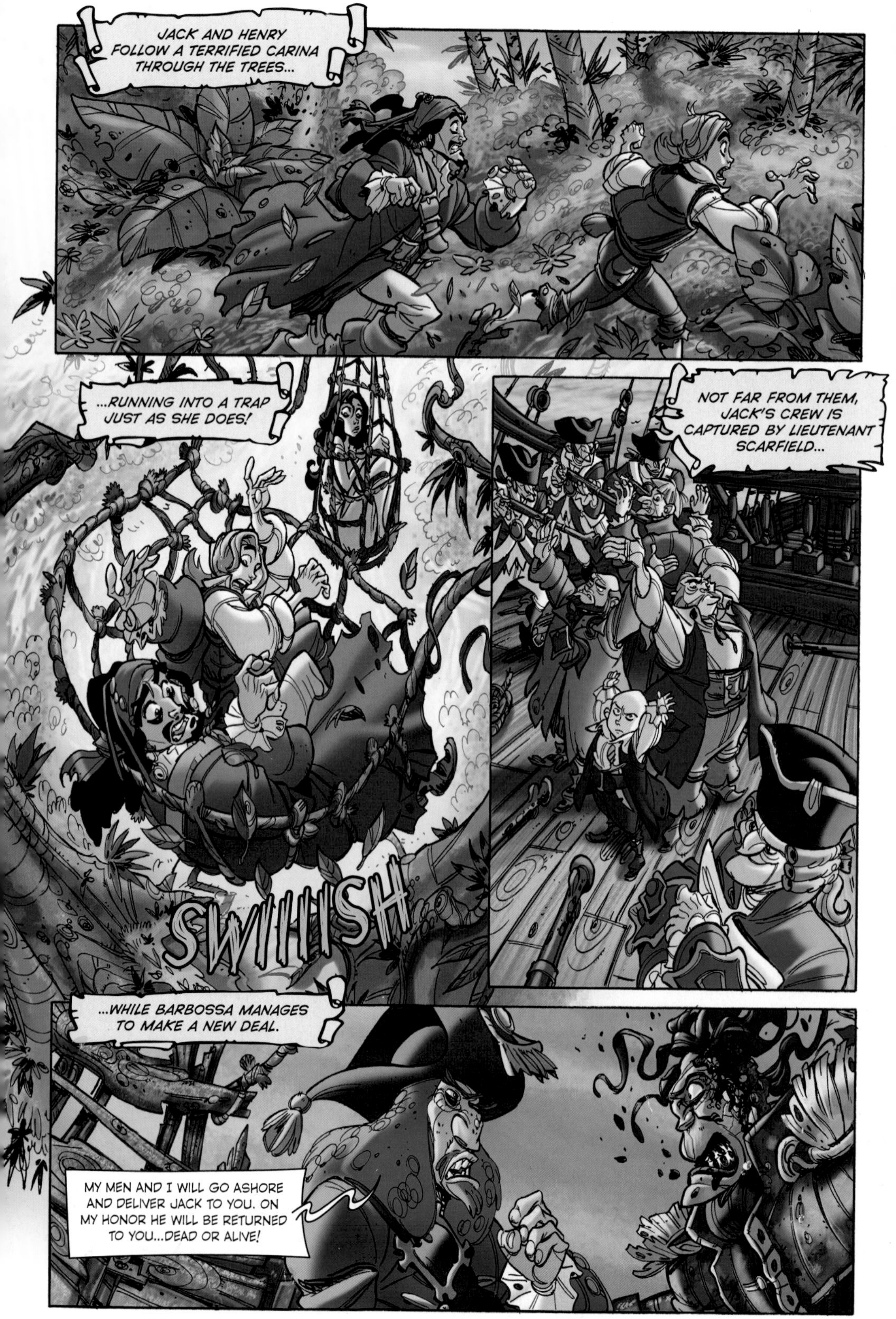
JACK AND HENRY FOLLOW A TERRIFIED CARINA THROUGH THE TREES...
...RUNNING INTO A TRAP JUST AS SHE DOES!
SWIIIISH
NOT FAR FROM THEM, JACK'S CREW IS CAPTURED BY LIEUTENANT SCARFIELD...
...WHILE BARBOSSA MANAGES TO MAKE A NEW DEAL.
MY MEN AND I WILL GO ASHORE AND DELIVER JACK TO YOU. ON MY HONOR HE WILL BE RETURNED TO YOU...DEAD OR ALIVE!

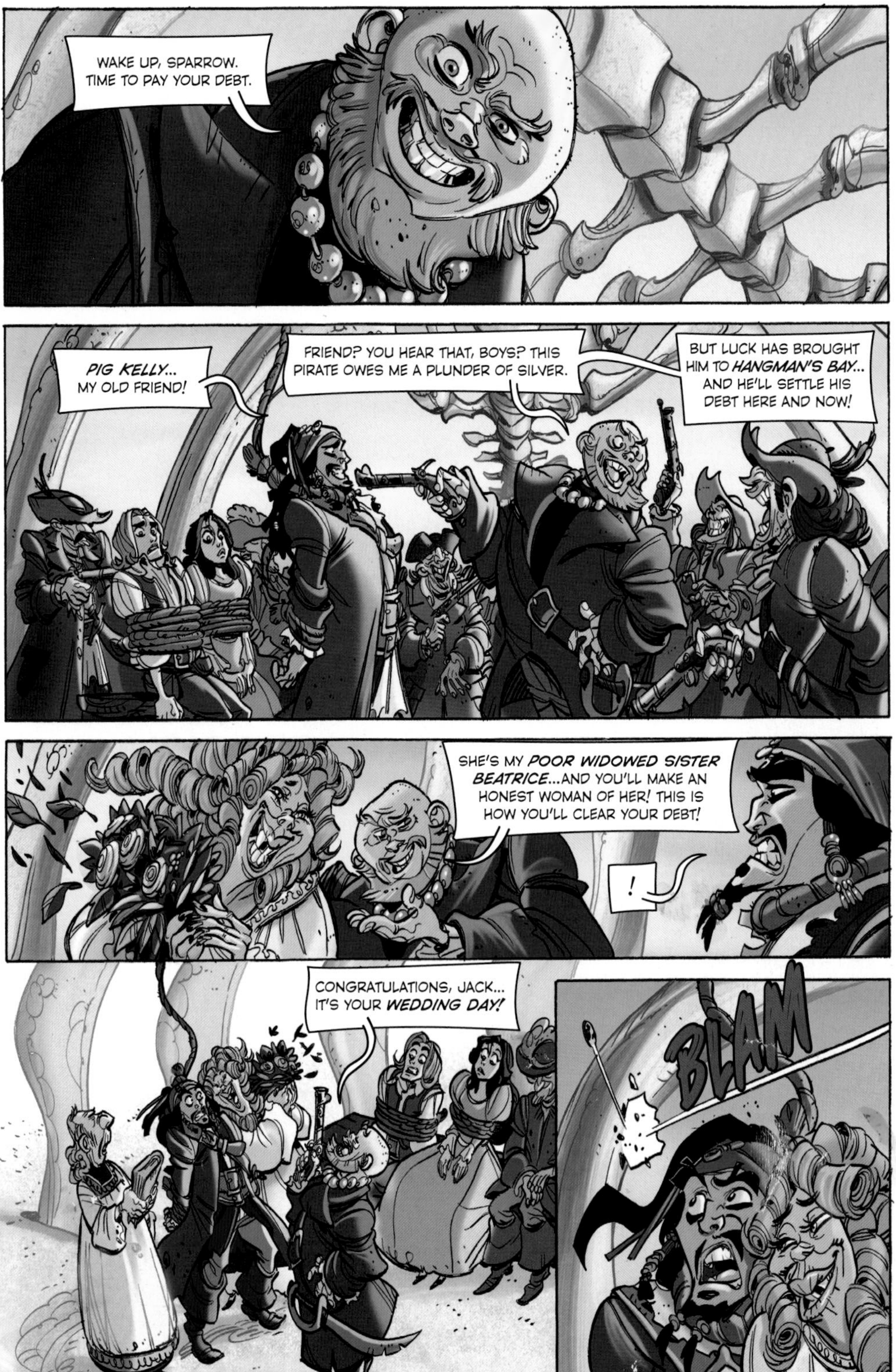
WAKE UP, SPARROW. TIME TO PAY YOUR DEBT.
PIG KELLY... MY OLD FRIEND!
FRIEND? YOU HEAR THAT, BOYS? THIS PIRATE OWES ME A PLUNDER OF SILVER.
BUT LUCK HAS BROUGHT HIM TO *HANGMAN'S BAY*... AND HE'LL SETTLE HIS DEBT HERE AND NOW!
SHE'S MY *POOR WIDOWED SISTER BEATRICE*...AND YOU'LL MAKE AN HONEST WOMAN OF HER! THIS IS HOW YOU'LL CLEAR YOUR DEBT!
!
CONGRATULATIONS, JACK... IT'S YOUR *WEDDING DAY!*
BLAM

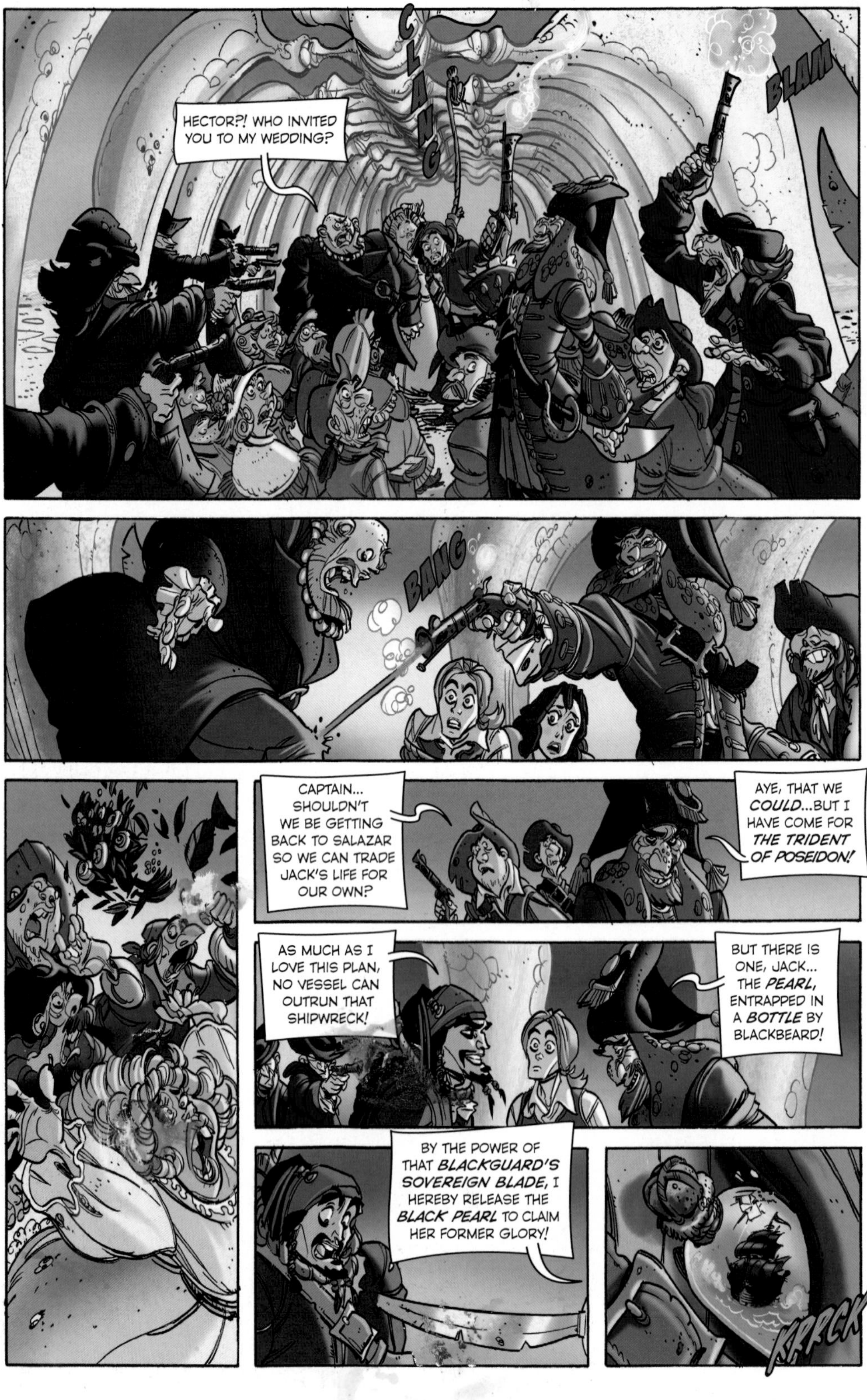
CLANG
BLAM
HECTOR?! WHO INVITED YOU TO MY WEDDING?
BANG
CAPTAIN... SHOULDN'T WE BE GETTING BACK TO SALAZAR SO WE CAN TRADE JACK'S LIFE FOR OUR OWN?
AYE, THAT WE COULD...BUT I HAVE COME FOR THE TRIDENT OF POSEIDON!
AS MUCH AS I LOVE THIS PLAN, NO VESSEL CAN OUTRUN THAT SHIPWRECK!
BUT THERE IS ONE, JACK... THE PEARL, ENTRAPPED IN A BOTTLE BY BLACKBEARD!
BY THE POWER OF THAT BLACKGUARD'S SOVEREIGN BLADE, I HEREBY RELEASE THE BLACK PEARL TO CLAIM HER FORMER GLORY!
KRRCK

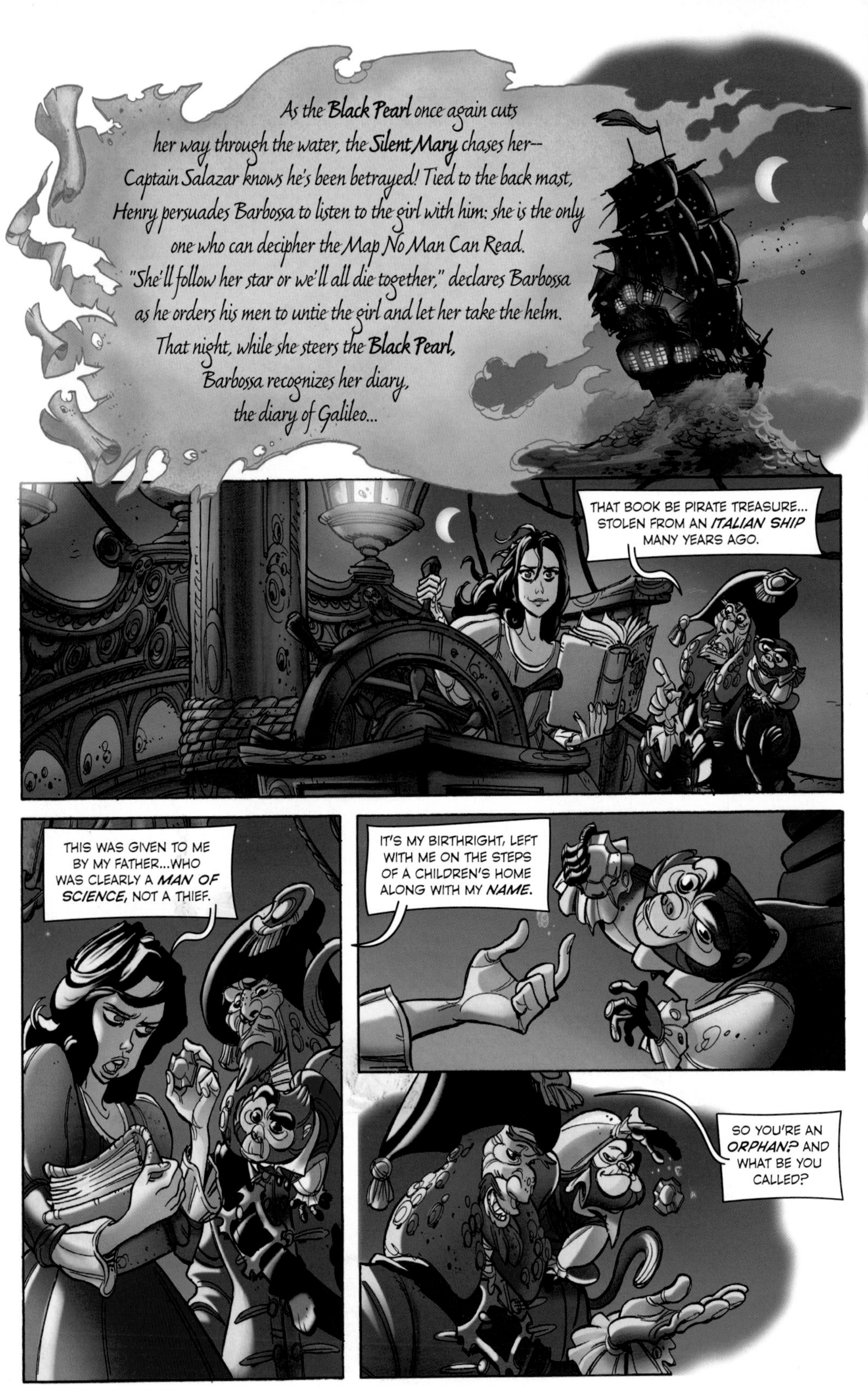
As the **Black Pearl** once again cuts
her way through the water, the **Silent Mary** chases her--
Captain Salazar knows he's been betrayed! Tied to the back mast,
Henry persuades Barbossa to listen to the girl with him: she is the only
one who can decipher the Map No Man Can Read.
"She'll follow her star or we'll all die together," declares Barbossa
as he orders his men to untie the girl and let her take the helm.
That night, while she steers the **Black Pearl**,
Barbossa recognizes her diary,
the diary of Galileo...
THAT BOOK BE PIRATE TREASURE... STOLEN FROM AN *ITALIAN SHIP* MANY YEARS AGO.
THIS WAS GIVEN TO ME BY MY FATHER...WHO WAS CLEARLY A ***MAN OF SCIENCE,*** NOT A THIEF.
IT'S MY BIRTHRIGHT, LEFT WITH ME ON THE STEPS OF A CHILDREN'S HOME ALONG WITH MY ***NAME.***
SO YOU'RE AN ***ORPHAN?*** AND WHAT BE YOU CALLED?

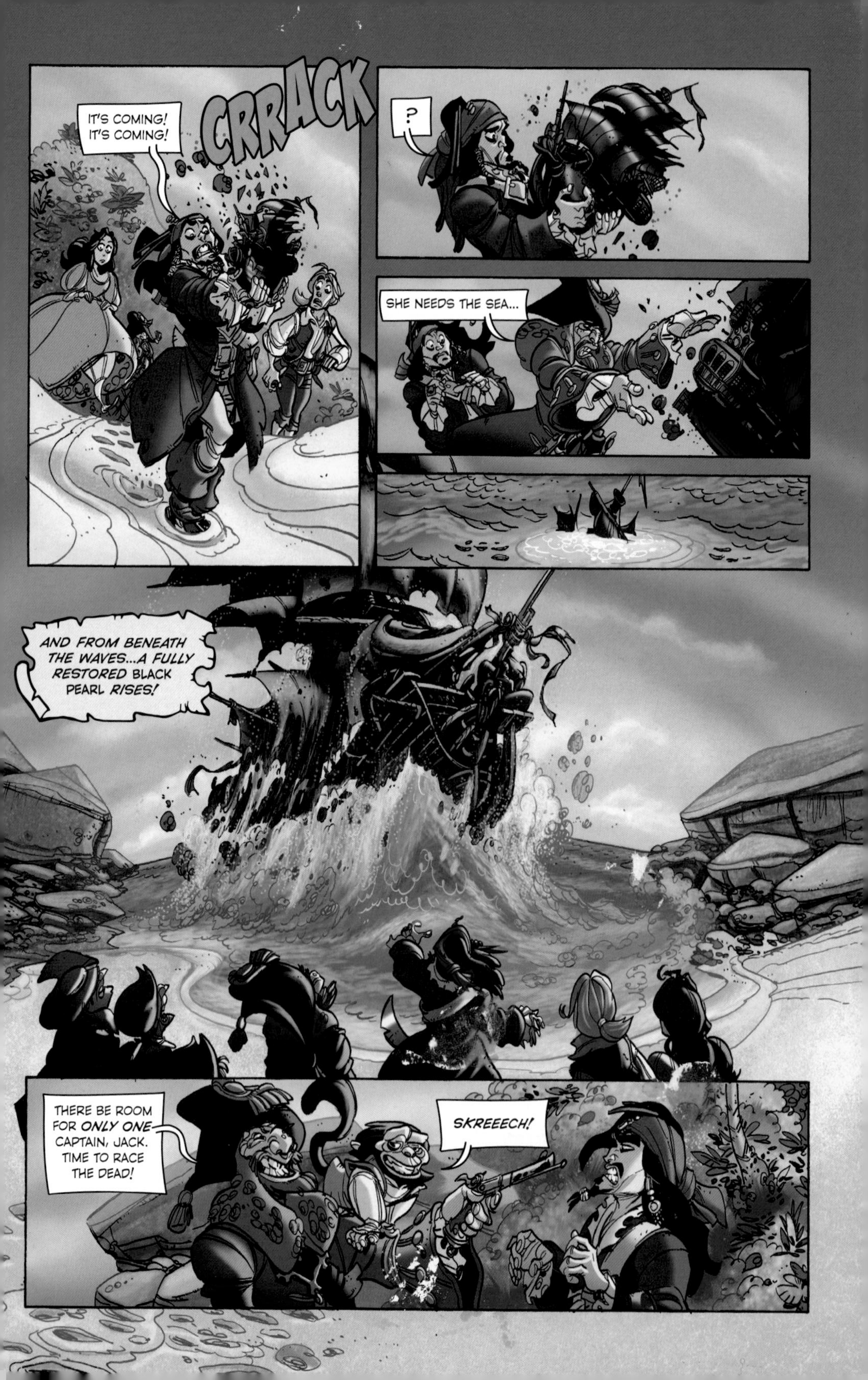
IT'S COMING! IT'S COMING!
CRRACK
?
SHE NEEDS THE SEA...
AND FROM BENEATH THE WAVES...A FULLY RESTORED BLACK PEARL RISES!
THERE BE ROOM FOR ONLY ONE CAPTAIN, JACK. TIME TO RACE THE DEAD!
SKREEECH!

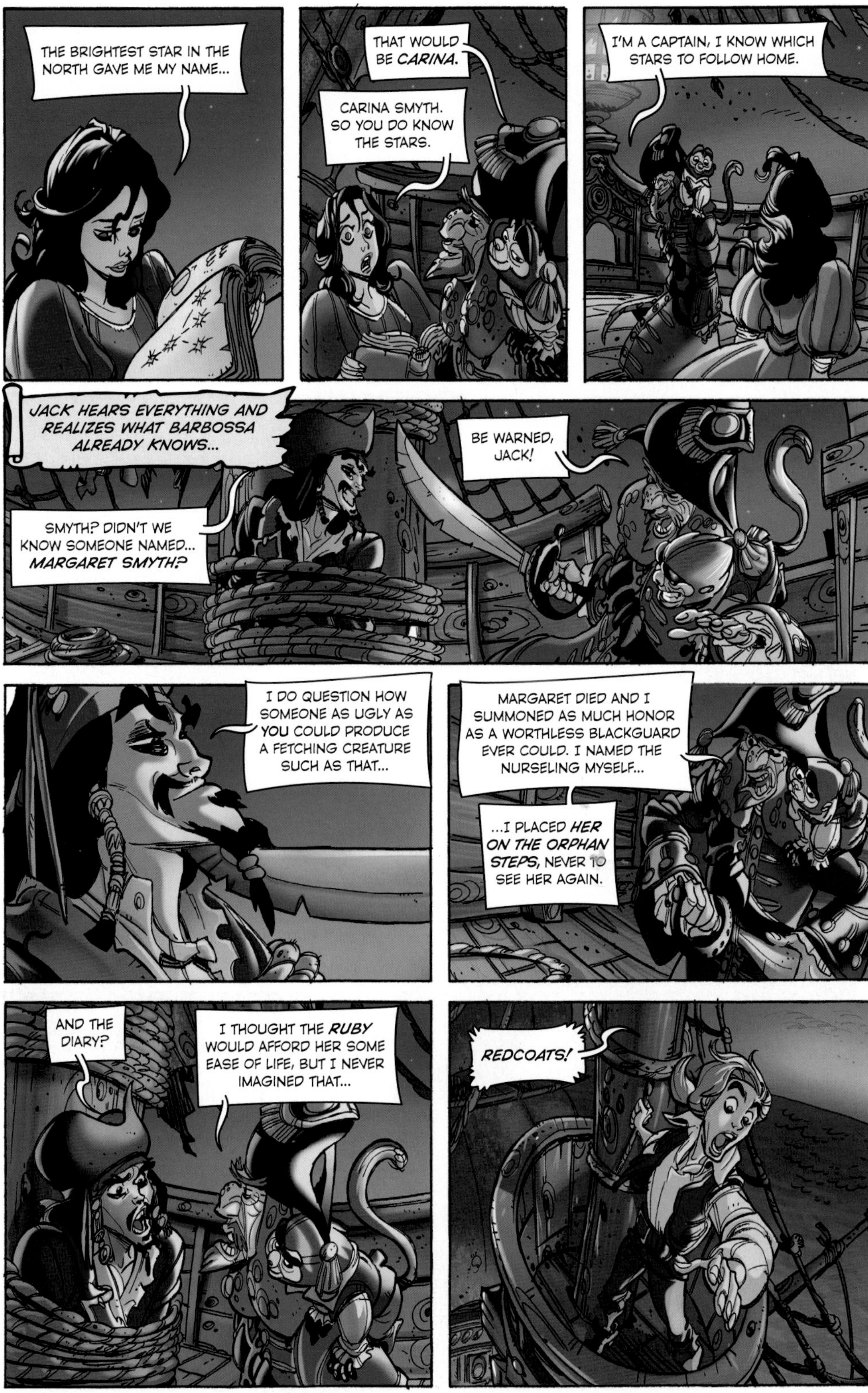
THE BRIGHTEST STAR IN THE NORTH GAVE ME MY NAME...
THAT WOULD BE *CARINA*.
CARINA SMYTH. SO YOU DO KNOW THE STARS.
I'M A CAPTAIN, I KNOW WHICH STARS TO FOLLOW HOME.
JACK HEARS EVERYTHING AND REALIZES WHAT BARBOSSA ALREADY KNOWS...
SMYTH? DIDN'T WE KNOW SOMEONE NAMED... *MARGARET SMYTH?*
BE WARNED, JACK!
I DO QUESTION HOW SOMEONE AS UGLY AS **YOU** COULD PRODUCE A FETCHING CREATURE SUCH AS THAT...
MARGARET DIED AND I SUMMONED AS MUCH HONOR AS A WORTHLESS BLACKGUARD EVER COULD. I NAMED THE NURSELING MYSELF...
...I PLACED *HER ON THE ORPHAN STEPS,* NEVER TO SEE HER AGAIN.
AND THE DIARY?
I THOUGHT THE *RUBY* WOULD AFFORD HER SOME EASE OF LIFE, BUT I NEVER IMAGINED THAT...
REDCOATS!

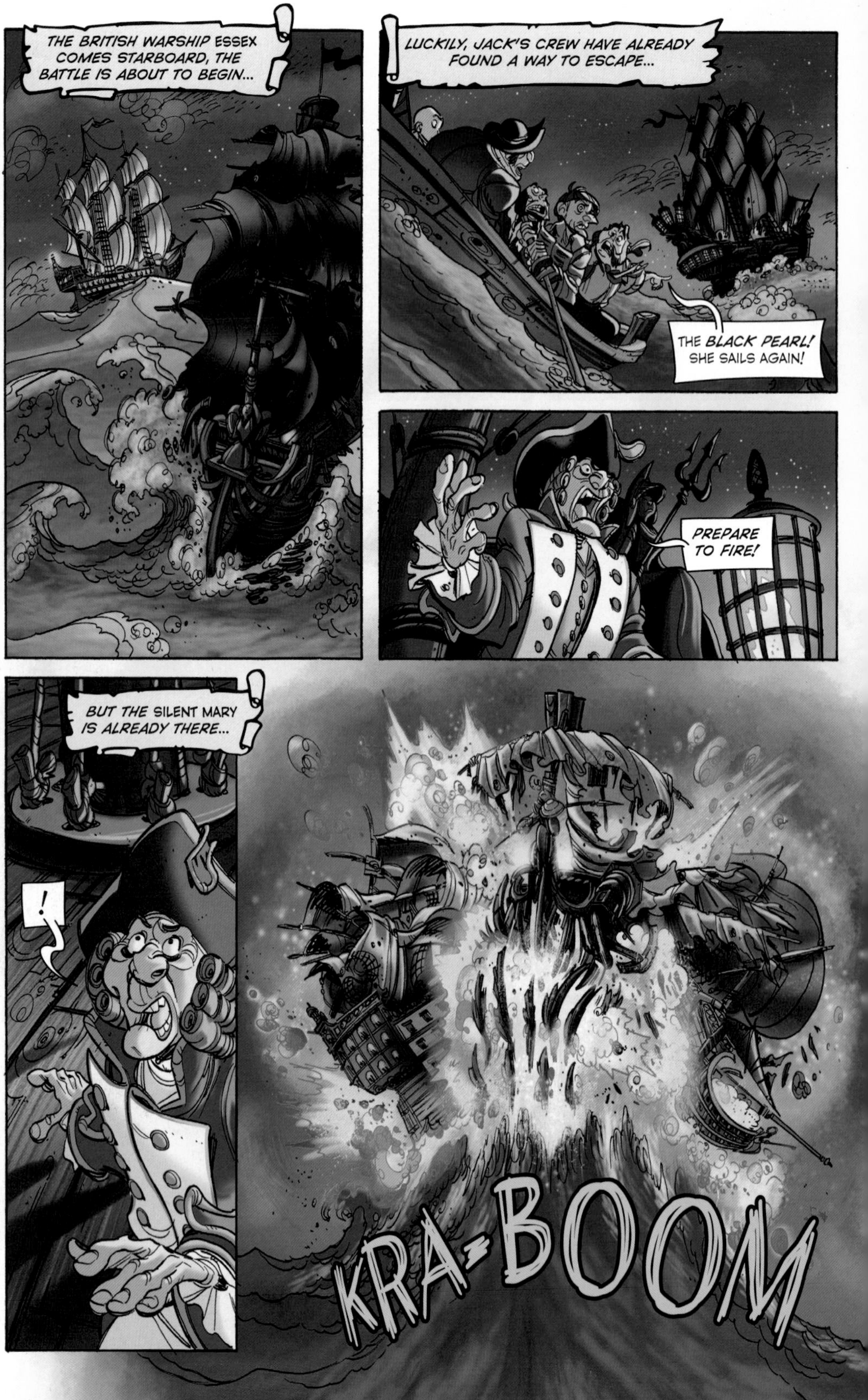
THE BRITISH WARSHIP ESSEX COMES STARBOARD, THE BATTLE IS ABOUT TO BEGIN...
LUCKILY, JACK'S CREW HAVE ALREADY FOUND A WAY TO ESCAPE...
THE BLACK PEARL! SHE SAILS AGAIN!
PREPARE TO FIRE!
BUT THE SILENT MARY IS ALREADY THERE...
!
KRA-BOOM

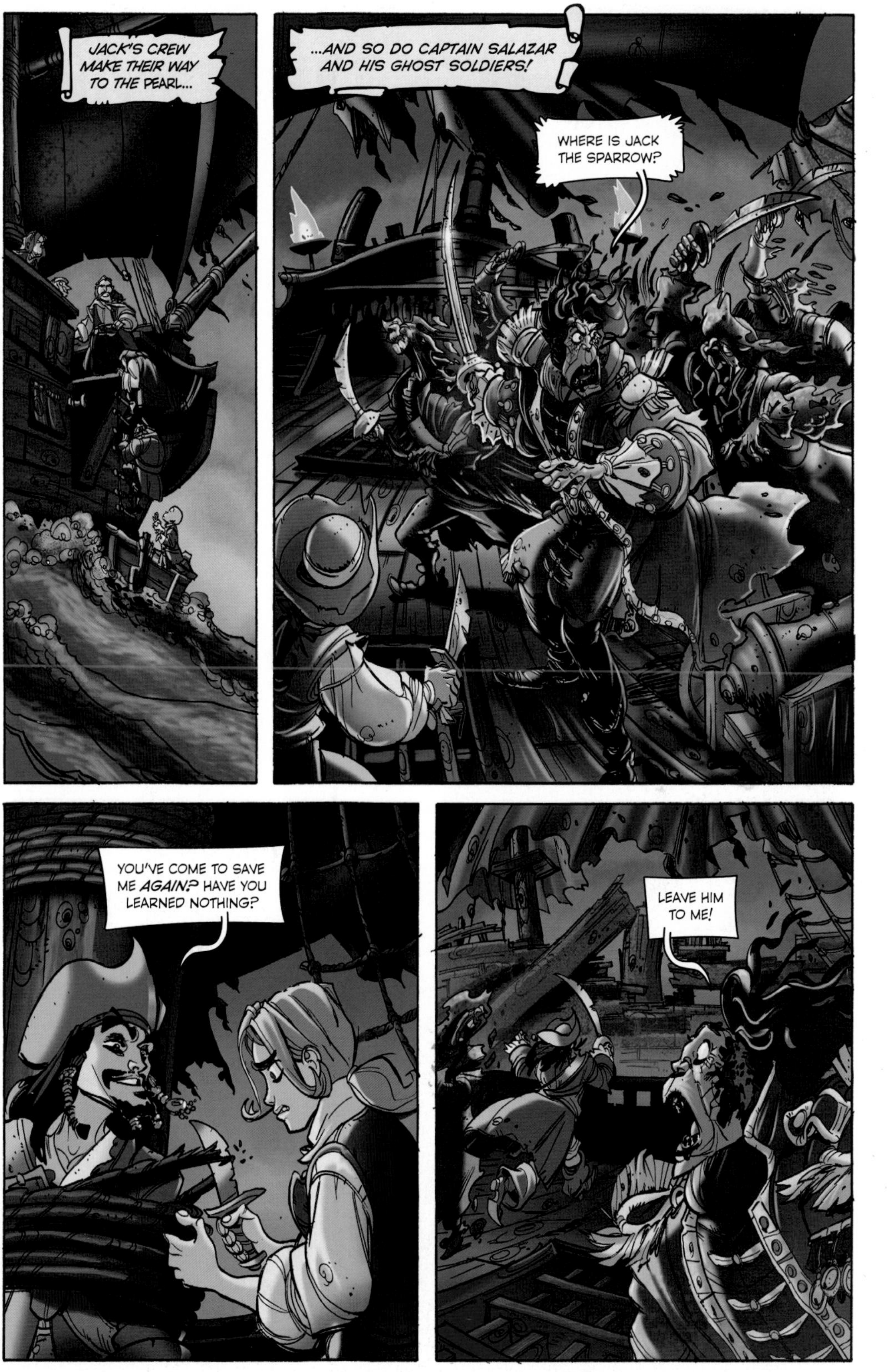
JACK'S CREW MAKE THEIR WAY TO THE PEARL...
...AND SO DO CAPTAIN SALAZAR AND HIS GHOST SOLDIERS!
WHERE IS JACK THE SPARROW?
YOU'VE COME TO SAVE ME *AGAIN?* HAVE YOU LEARNED NOTHING?
LEAVE HIM TO ME!

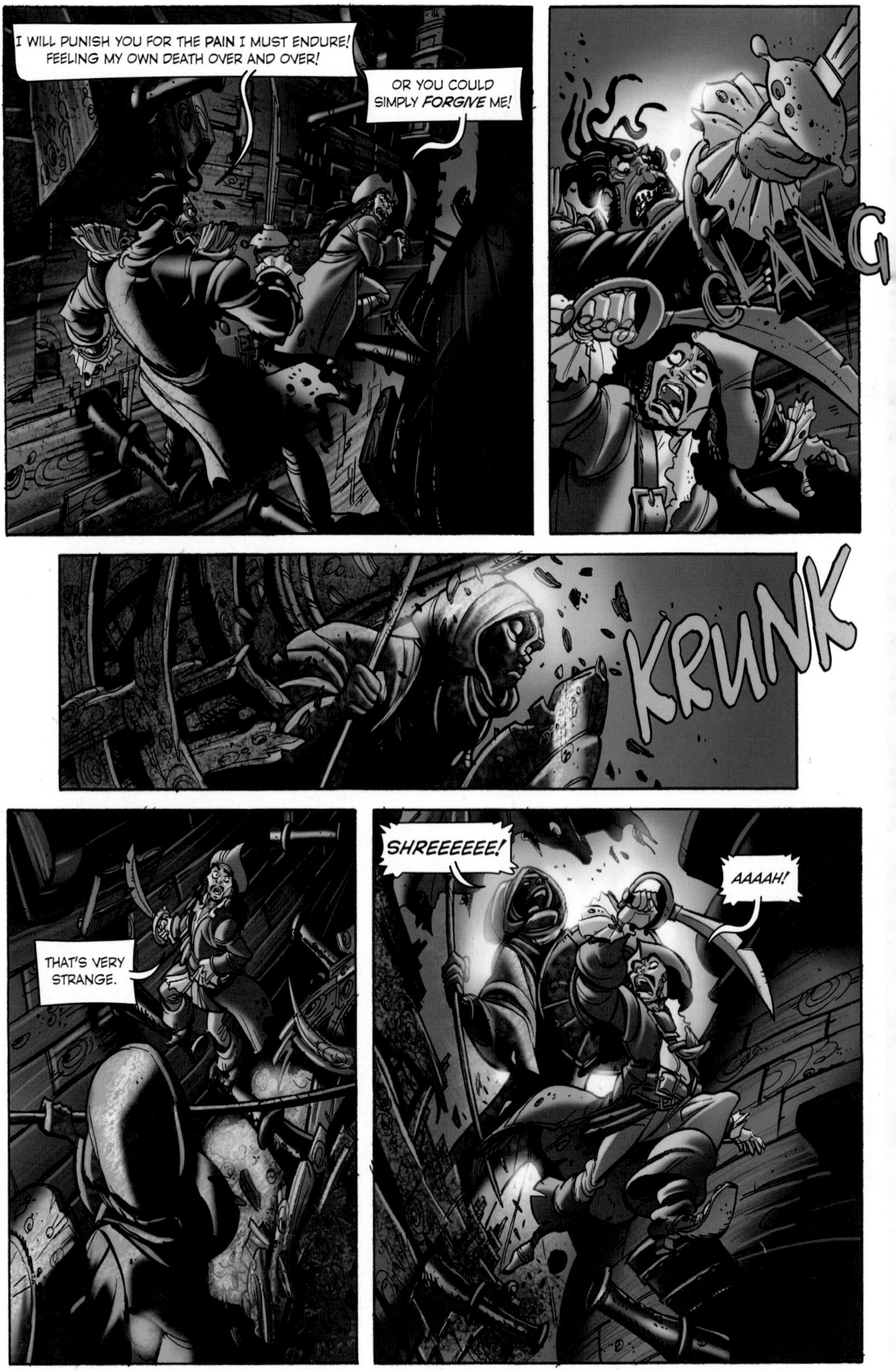
I WILL PUNISH YOU FOR THE PAIN I MUST ENDURE! FEELING MY OWN DEATH OVER AND OVER!
OR YOU COULD SIMPLY *FORGIVE* ME!
CLANG
KRUNK
THAT'S VERY STRANGE.
SHREEEEEE!
AAAAH!

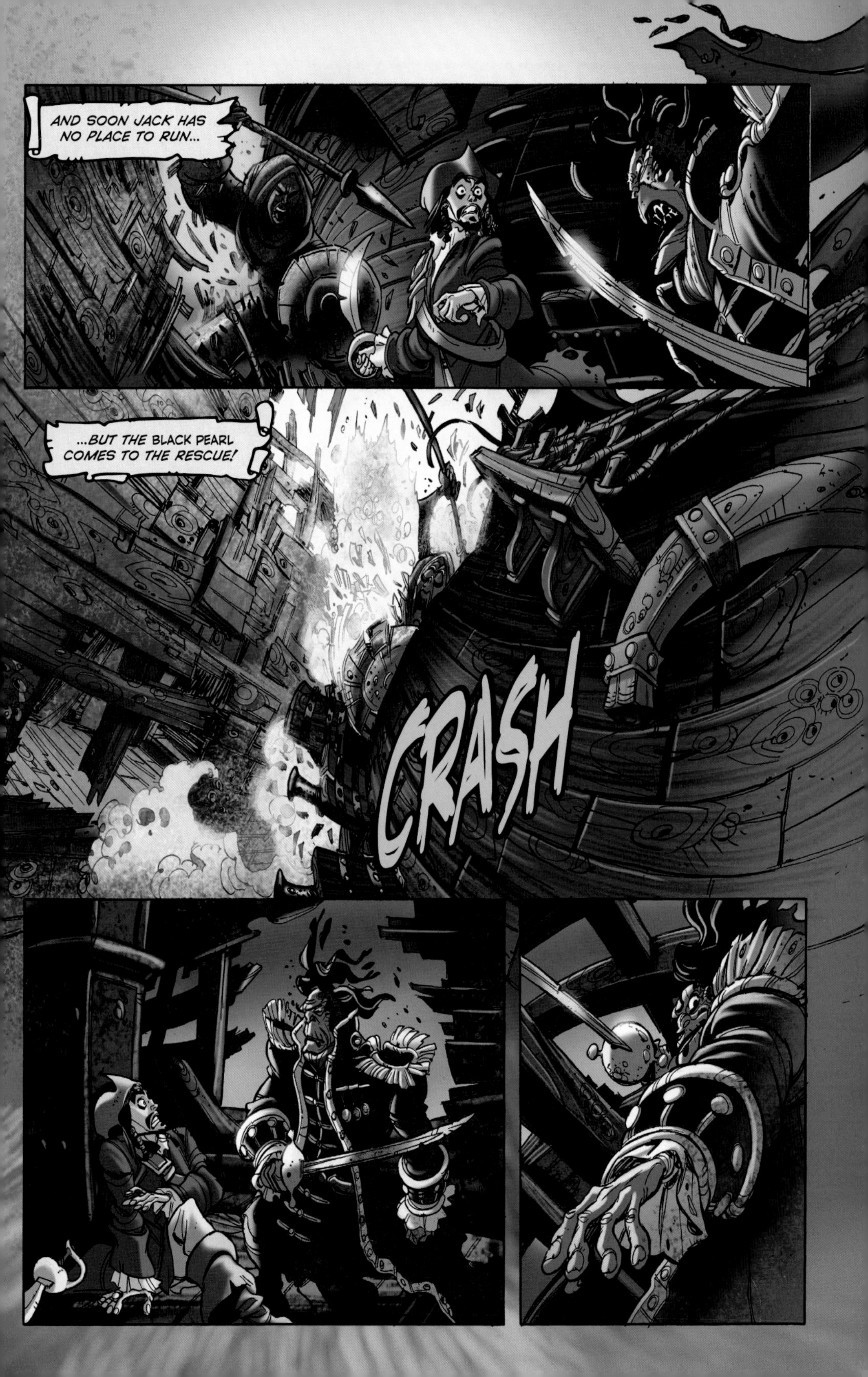
AND SOON JACK HAS NO PLACE TO RUN...
...BUT THE BLACK PEARL COMES TO THE RESCUE!
CRASH

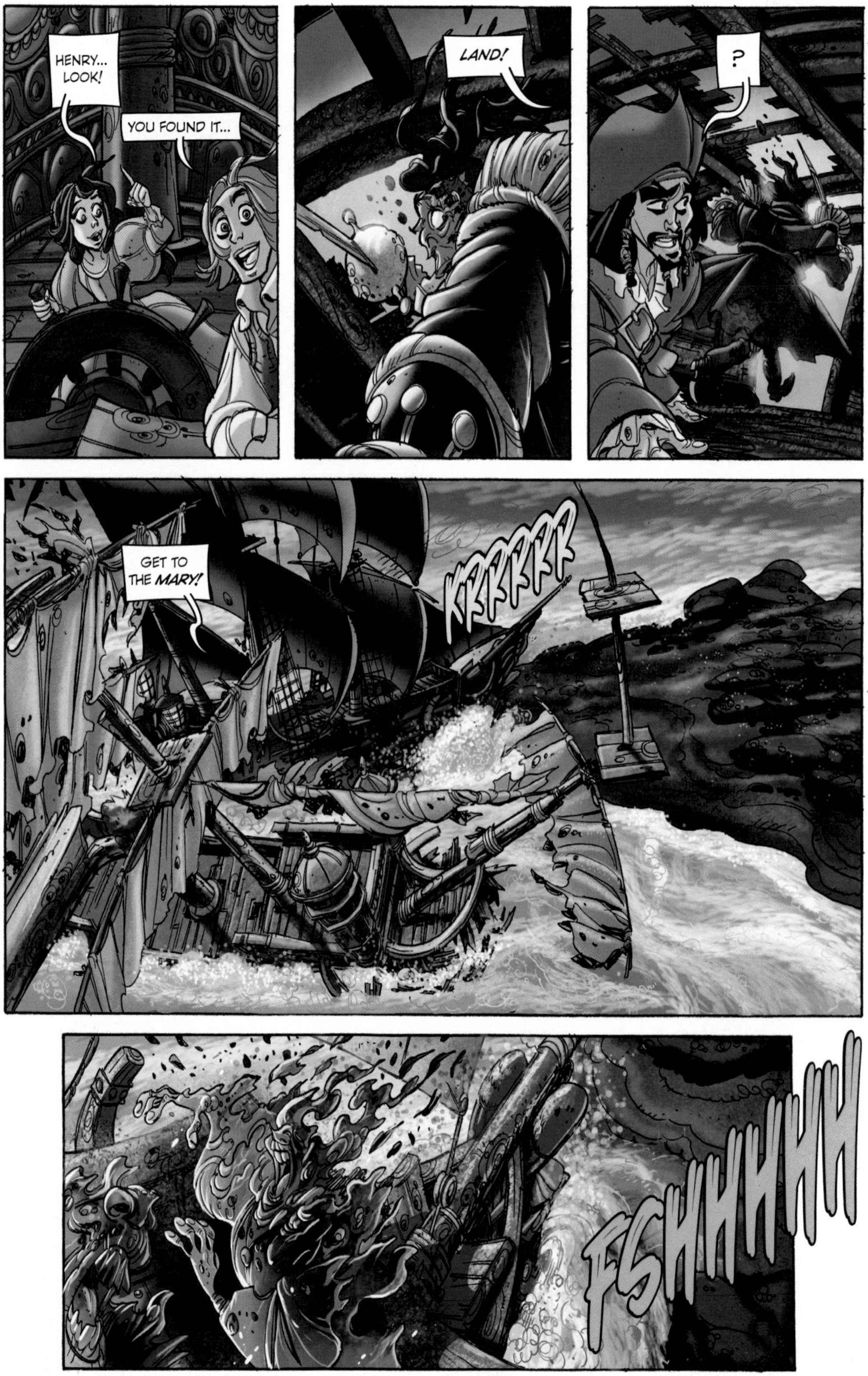
HENRY... LOOK!
YOU FOUND IT...
LAND!
?
GET TO THE MARY!
KRRRRR
FSHHHHHH

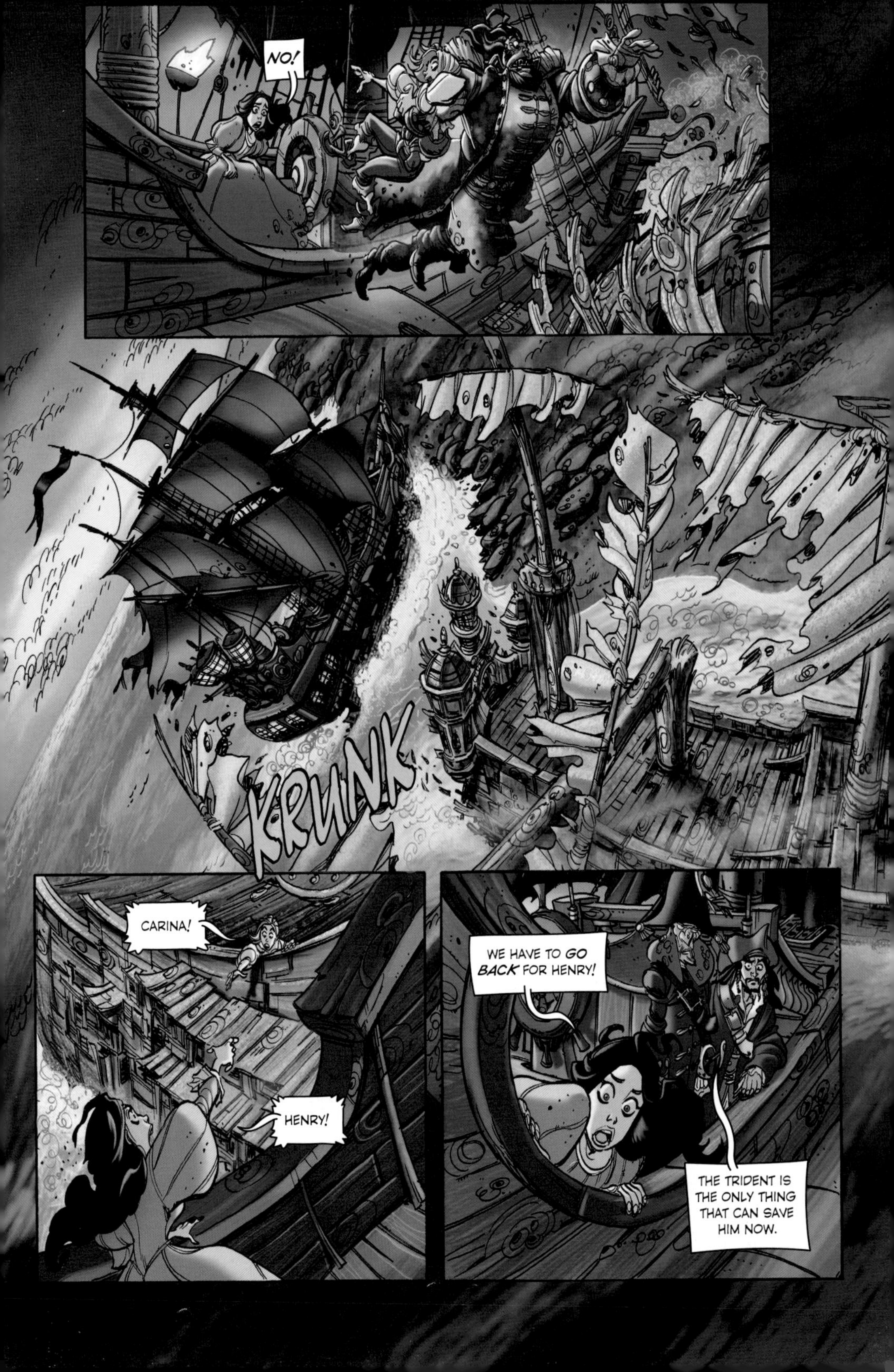
NO!
KRUNK
CARINA!
HENRY!
WE HAVE TO GO BACK FOR HENRY!
THE TRIDENT IS THE ONLY THING THAT CAN SAVE HIM NOW.

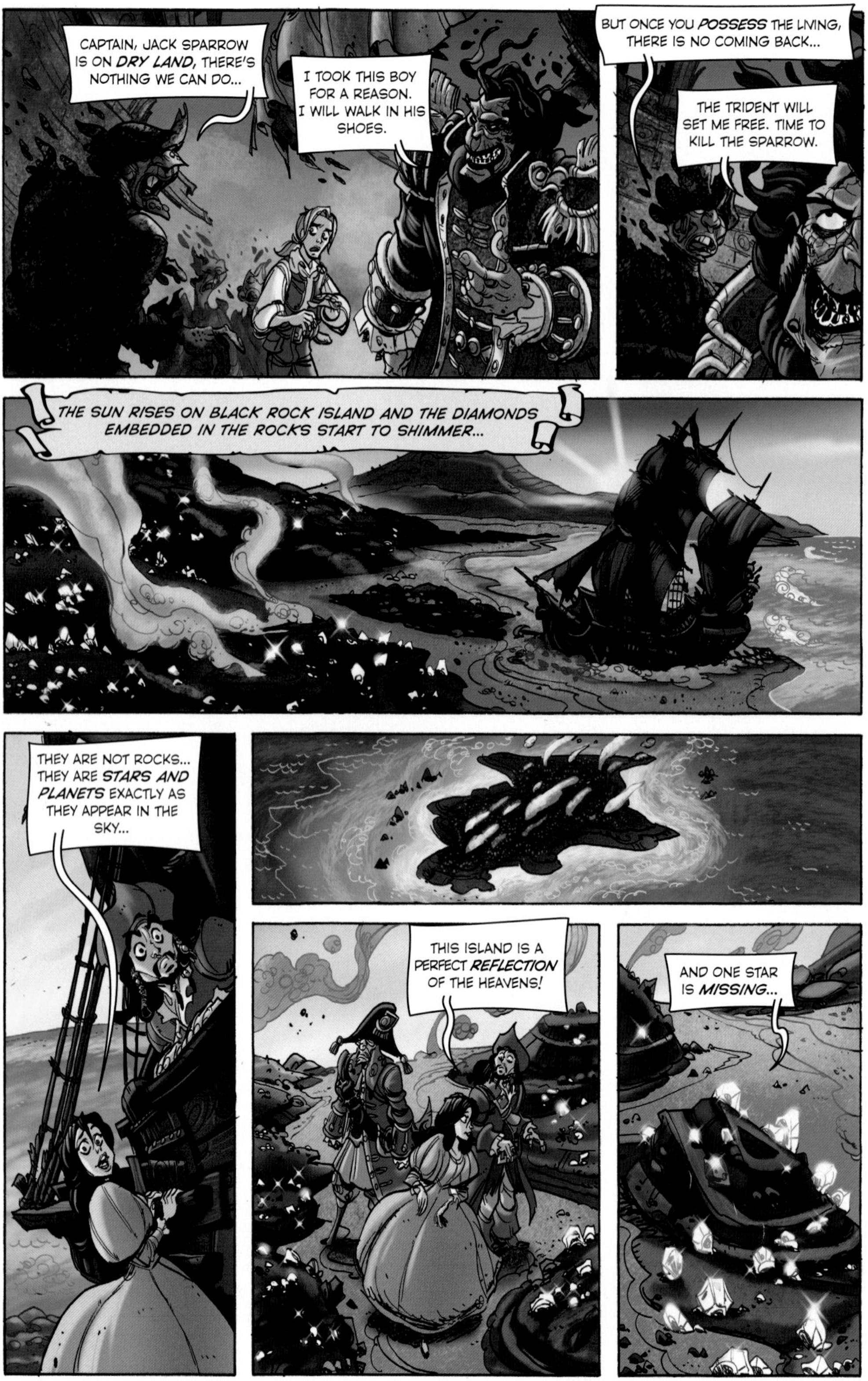
CAPTAIN, JACK SPARROW IS ON DRY LAND, THERE'S NOTHING WE CAN DO...
I TOOK THIS BOY FOR A REASON. I WILL WALK IN HIS SHOES.
BUT ONCE YOU POSSESS THE LIVING, THERE IS NO COMING BACK...
THE TRIDENT WILL SET ME FREE. TIME TO KILL THE SPARROW.
THE SUN RISES ON BLACK ROCK ISLAND AND THE DIAMONDS EMBEDDED IN THE ROCKS START TO SHIMMER...
THEY ARE NOT ROCKS... THEY ARE STARS AND PLANETS EXACTLY AS THEY APPEAR IN THE SKY...
THIS ISLAND IS A PERFECT REFLECTION OF THE HEAVENS!
AND ONE STAR IS MISSING...

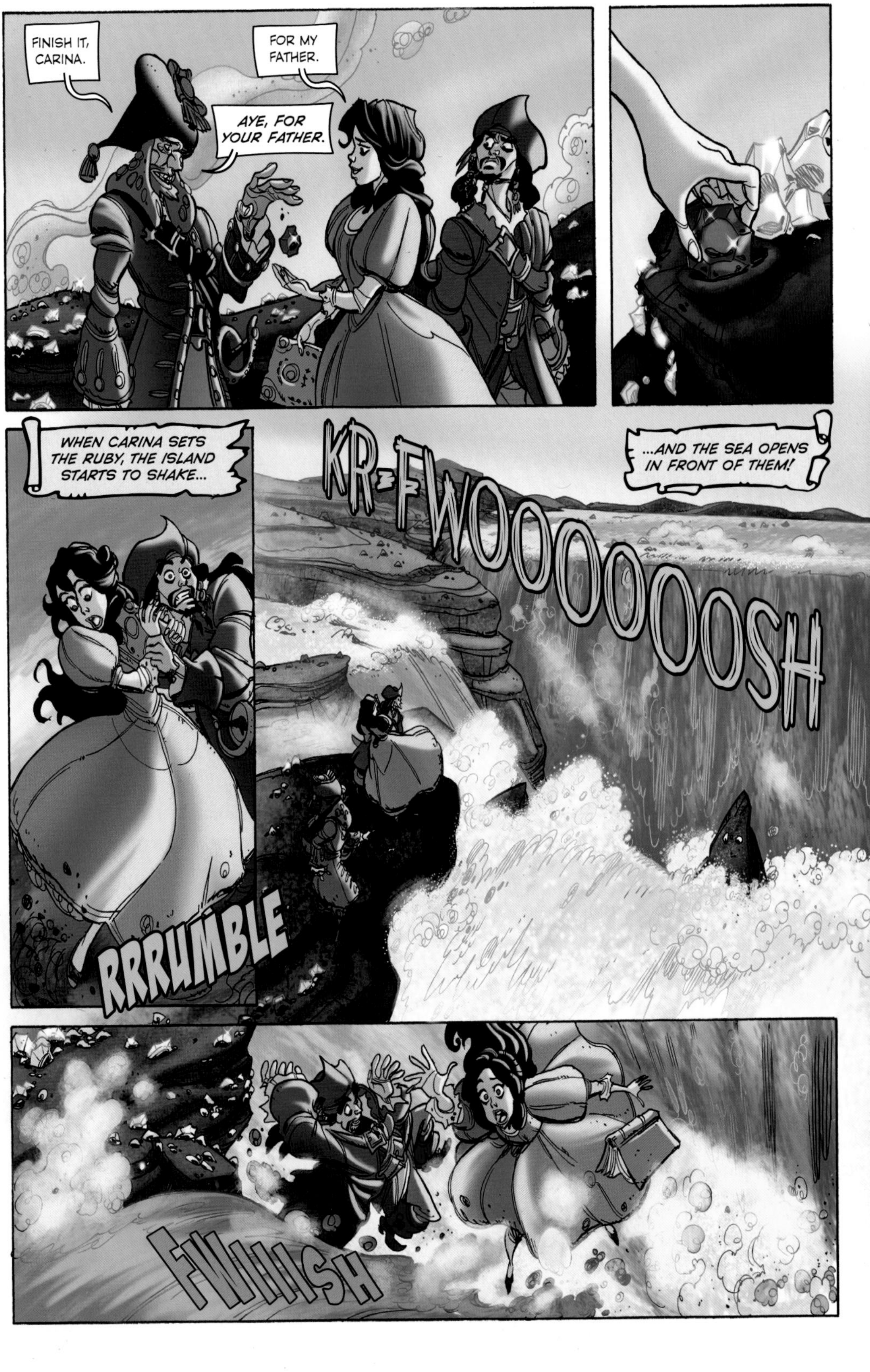
FINISH IT, CARINA.
FOR MY FATHER.
AYE, FOR YOUR FATHER.
WHEN CARINA SETS THE RUBY, THE ISLAND STARTS TO SHAKE...
KR-FWOOOOOOOOSH
...AND THE SEA OPENS IN FRONT OF THEM!
RRRUMBLE
FWIIIISH

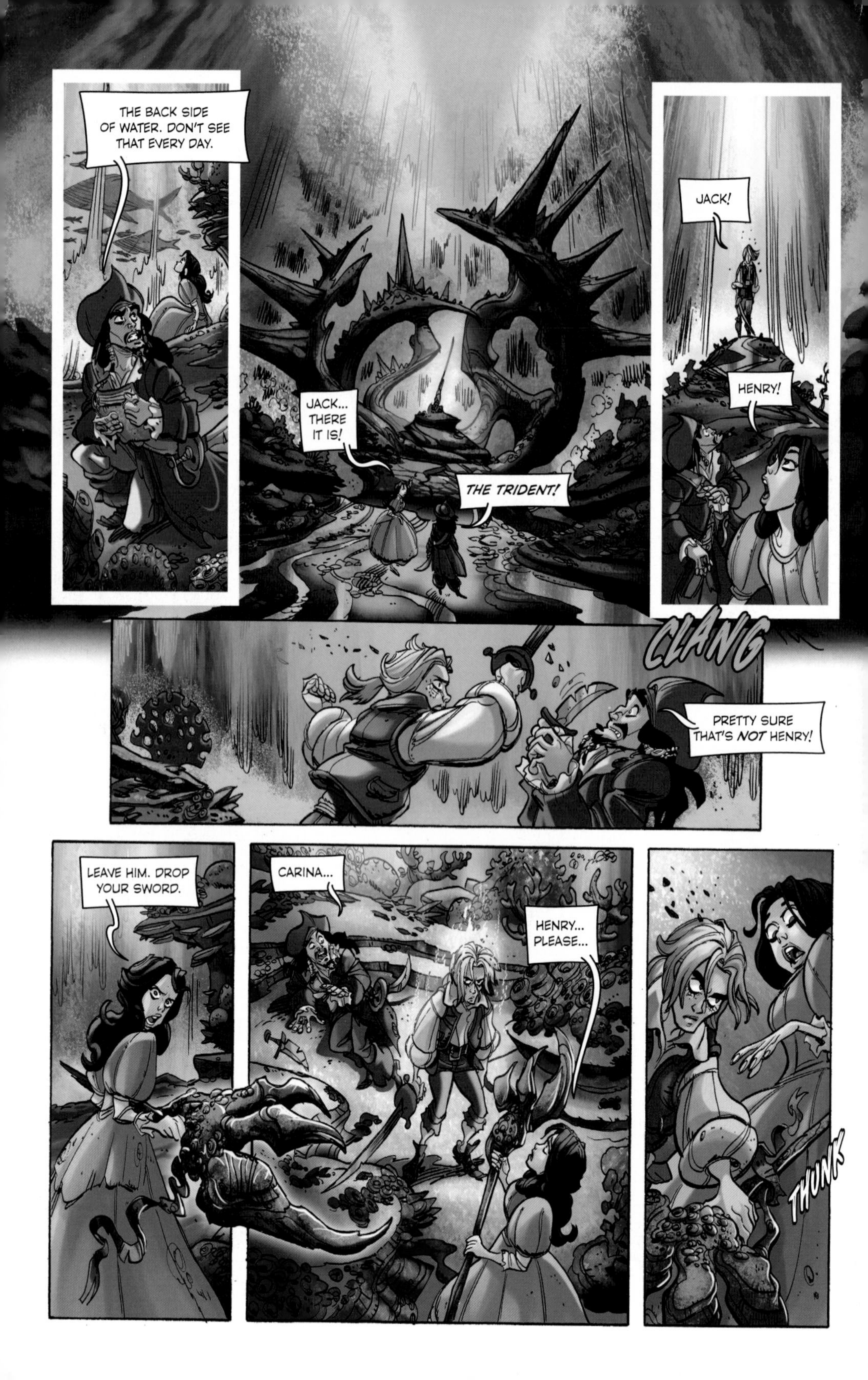
THE BACK SIDE OF WATER. DON'T SEE THAT EVERY DAY.
JACK... THERE IT IS!
THE TRIDENT!
JACK!
HENRY!
CLANG
PRETTY SURE THAT'S *NOT* HENRY!
LEAVE HIM. DROP YOUR SWORD.
CARINA...
HENRY... PLEASE...
THUNK

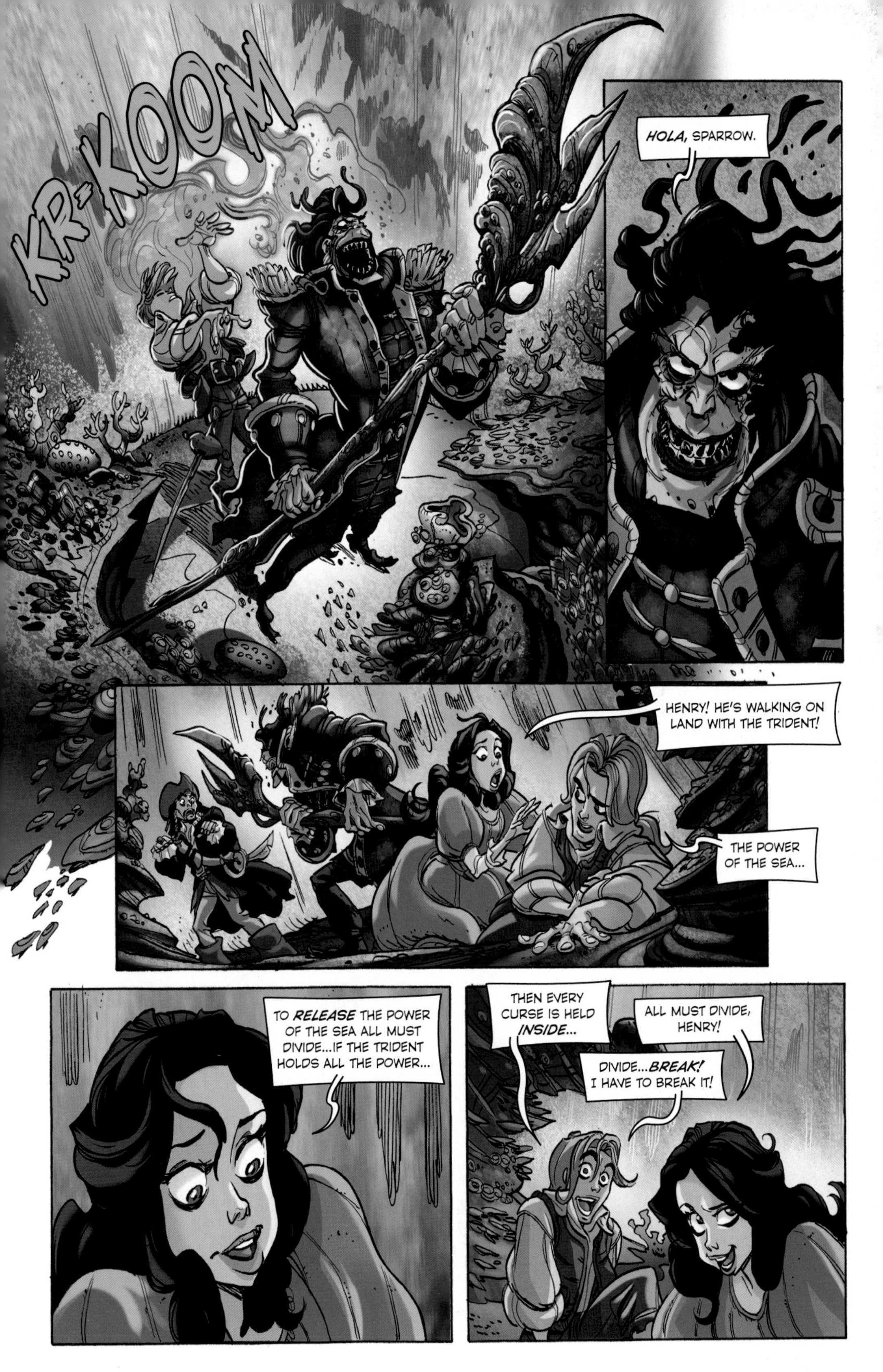
KR-KOOM
HOLA, SPARROW.
HENRY! HE'S WALKING ON LAND WITH THE TRIDENT!
THE POWER OF THE SEA...
TO RELEASE THE POWER OF THE SEA ALL MUST DIVIDE...IF THE TRIDENT HOLDS ALL THE POWER...
THEN EVERY CURSE IS HELD INSIDE...
ALL MUST DIVIDE, HENRY!
DIVIDE...BREAK! I HAVE TO BREAK IT!

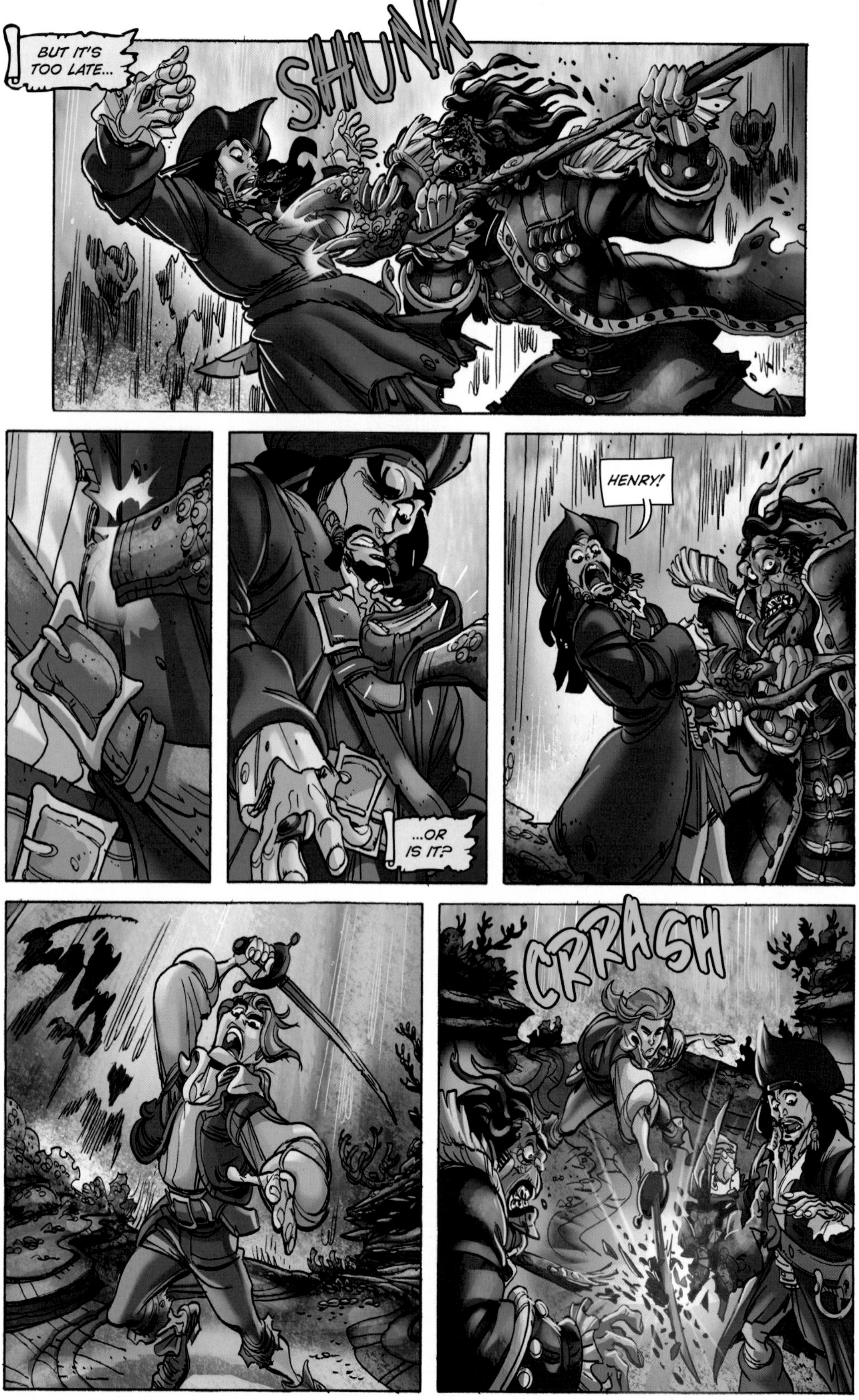

BUT IT'S TOO LATE...
SHUNK
...OR IS IT?
HENRY!
CRRASH

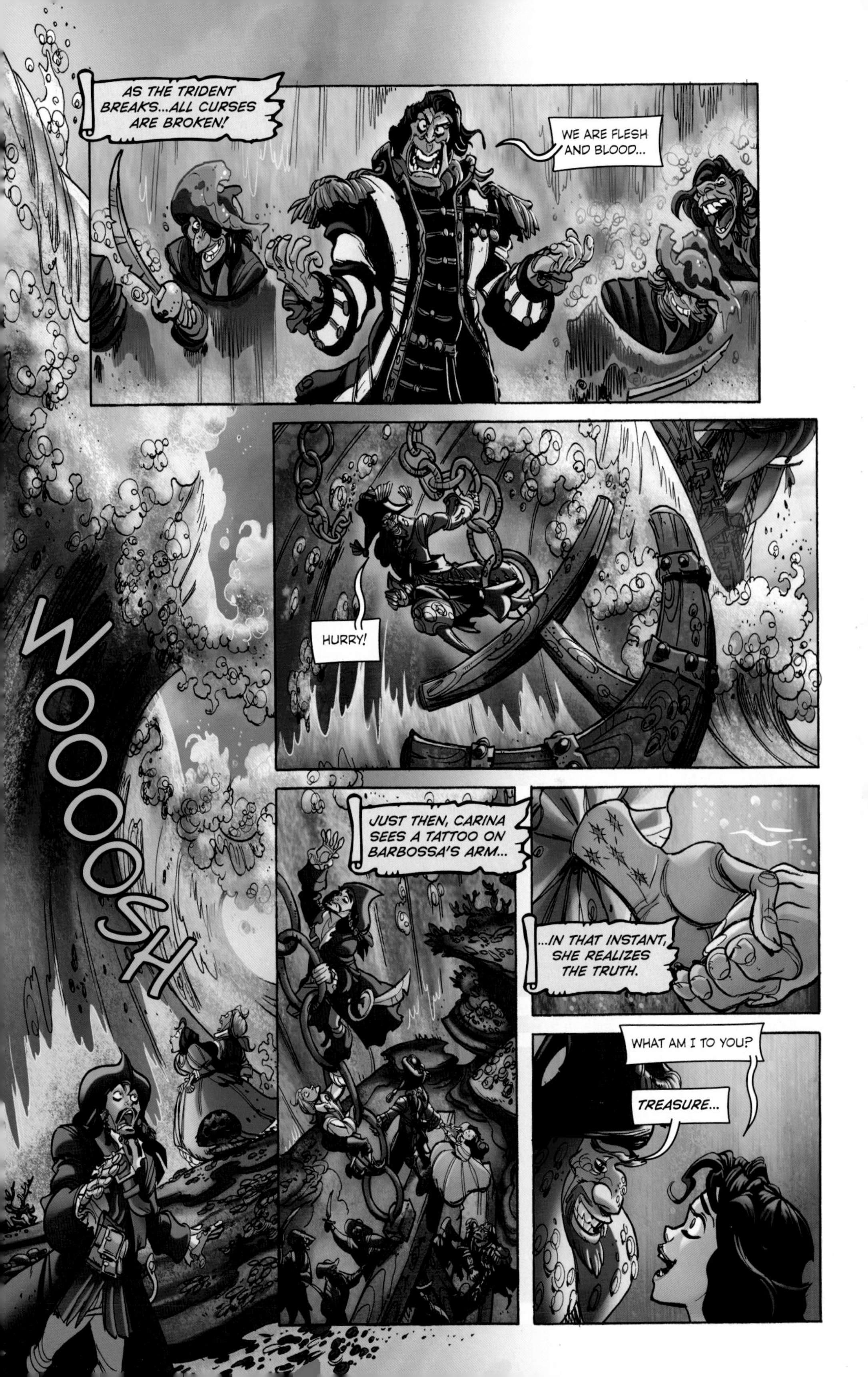
AS THE TRIDENT BREAKS...ALL CURSES ARE BROKEN!
WE ARE FLESH AND BLOOD...
HURRY!
WOOOOSH
JUST THEN, CARINA SEES A TATTOO ON BARBOSSA'S ARM...
...IN THAT INSTANT, SHE REALIZES THE TRUTH.
WHAT AM I TO YOU?
TREASURE...

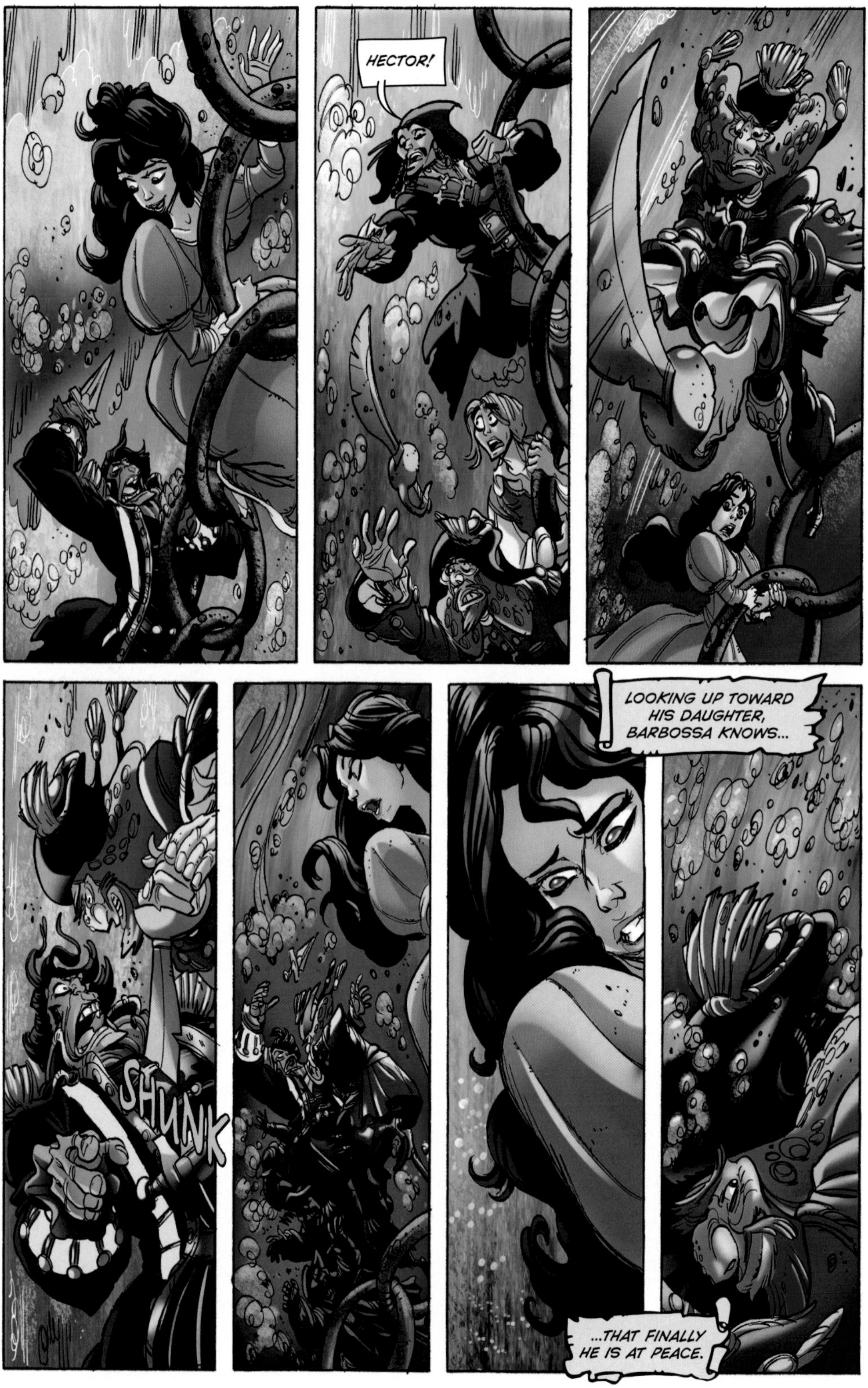
HECTOR!
LOOKING UP TOWARD HIS DAUGHTER, BARBOSSA KNOWS...
SHUNK
...THAT FINALLY HE IS AT PEACE.

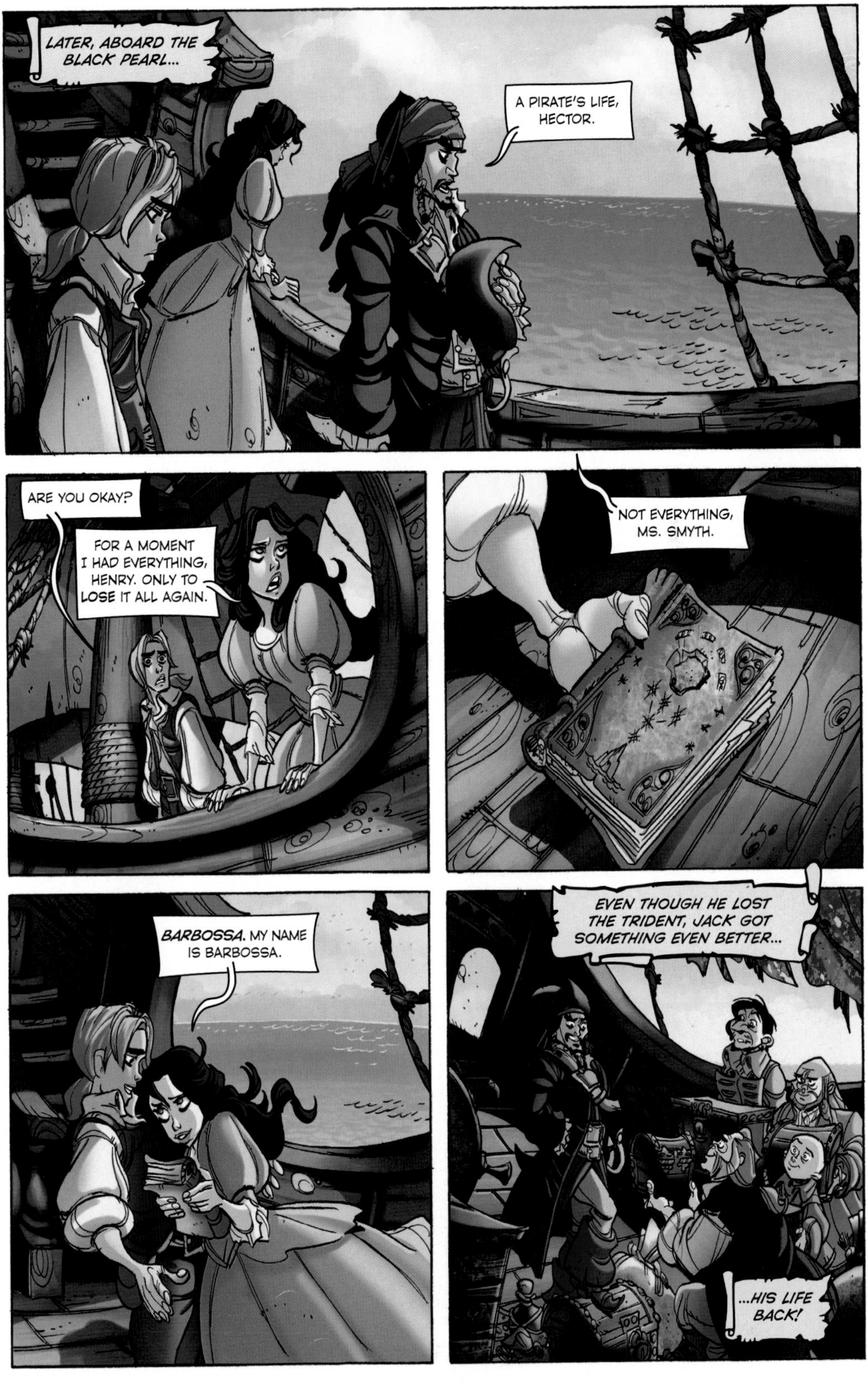
LATER, ABOARD THE BLACK PEARL...
A PIRATE'S LIFE, HECTOR.
ARE YOU OKAY?
FOR A MOMENT I HAD EVERYTHING, HENRY. ONLY TO LOSE IT ALL AGAIN.
NOT EVERYTHING, MS. SMYTH.
BARBOSSA. MY NAME IS BARBOSSA.
EVEN THOUGH HE LOST THE TRIDENT, JACK GOT SOMETHING EVEN BETTER...
...HIS LIFE BACK!

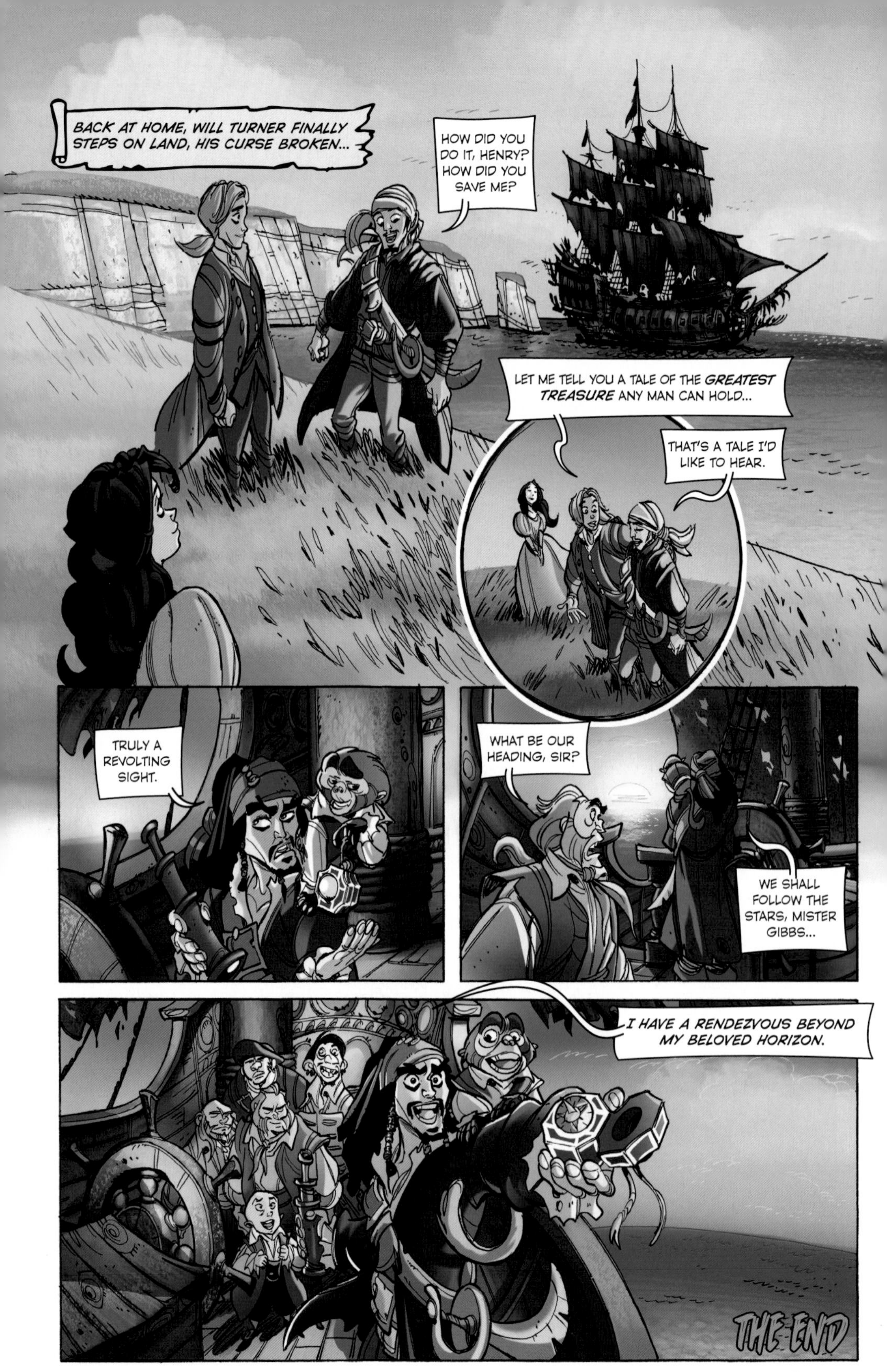
BACK AT HOME, WILL TURNER FINALLY STEPS ON LAND, HIS CURSE BROKEN...
HOW DID YOU DO IT, HENRY? HOW DID YOU SAVE ME?
LET ME TELL YOU A TALE OF THE *GREATEST TREASURE* ANY MAN CAN HOLD...
THAT'S A TALE I'D LIKE TO HEAR.
TRULY A REVOLTING SIGHT.
WHAT BE OUR HEADING, SIR?
WE SHALL FOLLOW THE STARS, MISTER GIBBS...
I HAVE A RENDEZVOUS BEYOND MY BELOVED HORIZON.
THE END

The Secret of Galileo's Diary

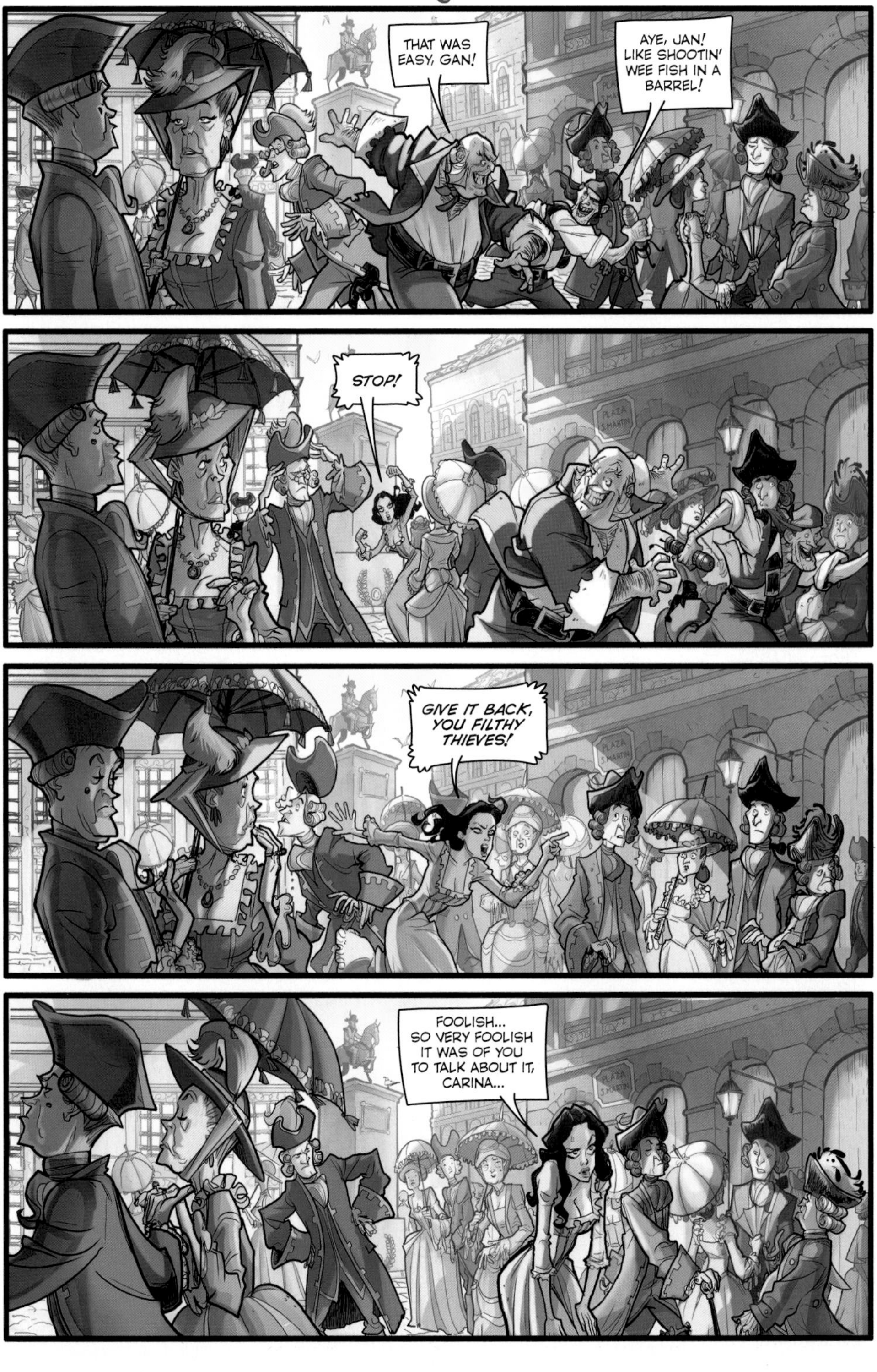

THAT WAS EASY, GAN!
AYE, JAN! LIKE SHOOTIN' WEE FISH IN A BARREL!
STOP!
GIVE IT BACK, YOU FILTHY THIEVES!
FOOLISH... SO VERY FOOLISH IT WAS OF YOU TO TALK ABOUT IT, CARINA...

Script: Alessandro Ferrari • Layouts & Pencils: Lelio Bonaccorso • Inks: Igor Chimisso • Colors: Kawaii Creative Studio • Letters: Chris Dickey

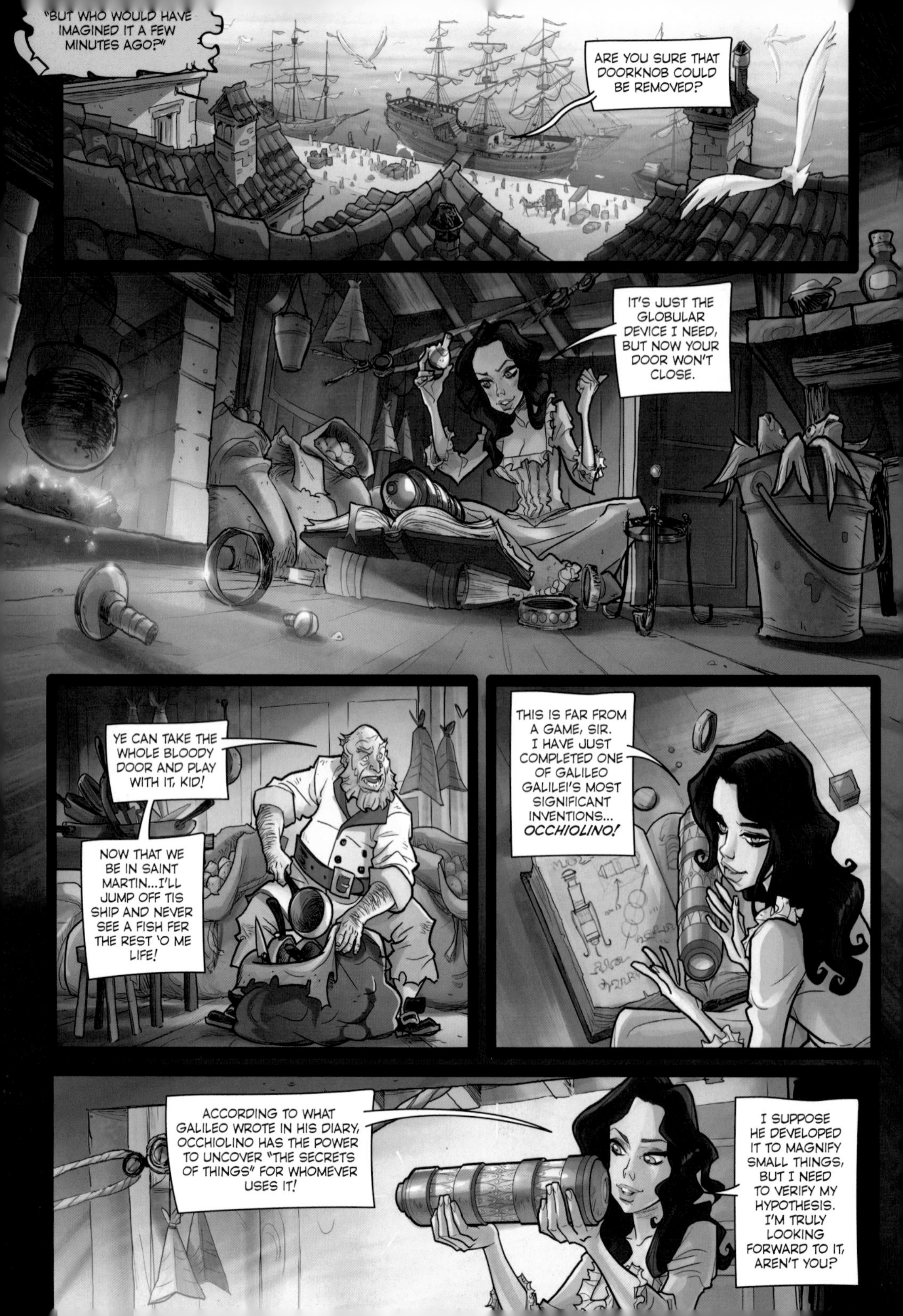
"BUT WHO WOULD HAVE IMAGINED IT A FEW MINUTES AGO?"
ARE YOU SURE THAT DOORKNOB COULD BE REMOVED?
IT'S JUST THE GLOBULAR DEVICE I NEED, BUT NOW YOUR DOOR WON'T CLOSE.
YE CAN TAKE THE WHOLE BLOODY DOOR AND PLAY WITH IT, KID!
NOW THAT WE BE IN SAINT MARTIN...I'LL JUMP OFF TIS SHIP AND NEVER SEE A FISH FER THE REST 'O ME LIFE!
THIS IS FAR FROM A GAME, SIR. I HAVE JUST COMPLETED ONE OF GALILEO GALILEI'S MOST SIGNIFICANT INVENTIONS... *OCCHIOLINO!*
ACCORDING TO WHAT GALILEO WROTE IN HIS DIARY, OCCHIOLINO HAS THE POWER TO UNCOVER "THE SECRETS OF THINGS" FOR WHOMEVER USES IT!
I SUPPOSE HE DEVELOPED IT TO MAGNIFY SMALL THINGS, BUT I NEED TO VERIFY MY HYPOTHESIS. I'M TRULY LOOKING FORWARD TO IT, AREN'T YOU?

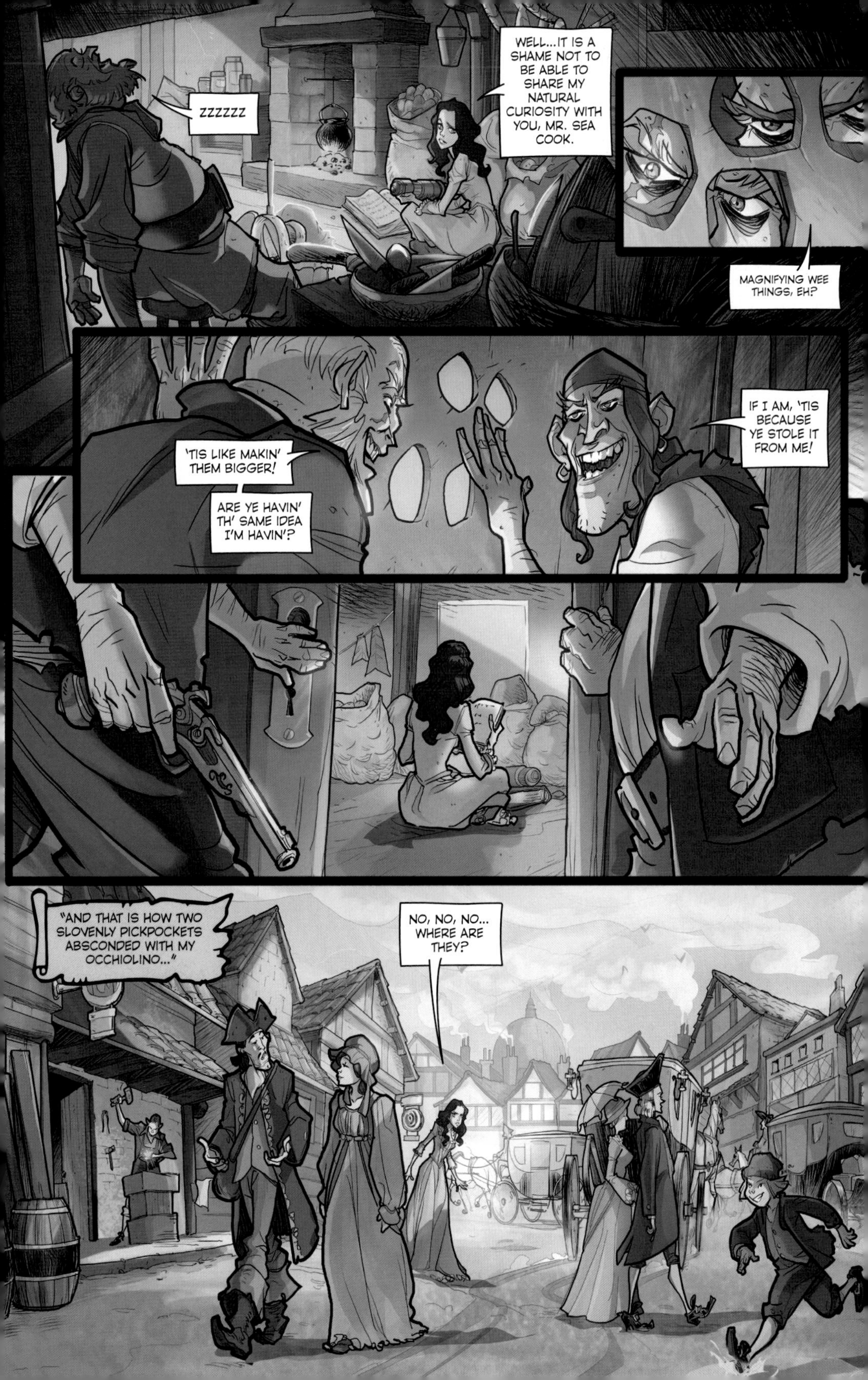
ZZZZZZ
WELL...IT IS A SHAME NOT TO BE ABLE TO SHARE MY NATURAL CURIOSITY WITH YOU, MR. SEA COOK.
MAGNIFYING WEE THINGS, EH?
'TIS LIKE MAKIN' THEM BIGGER!
ARE YE HAVIN' TH' SAME IDEA I'M HAVIN'?
IF I AM, 'TIS BECAUSE YE STOLE IT FROM ME!
"AND THAT IS HOW TWO SLOVENLY PICKPOCKETS ABSCONDED WITH MY OCCHIOLINO..."
NO, NO, NO... WHERE ARE THEY?

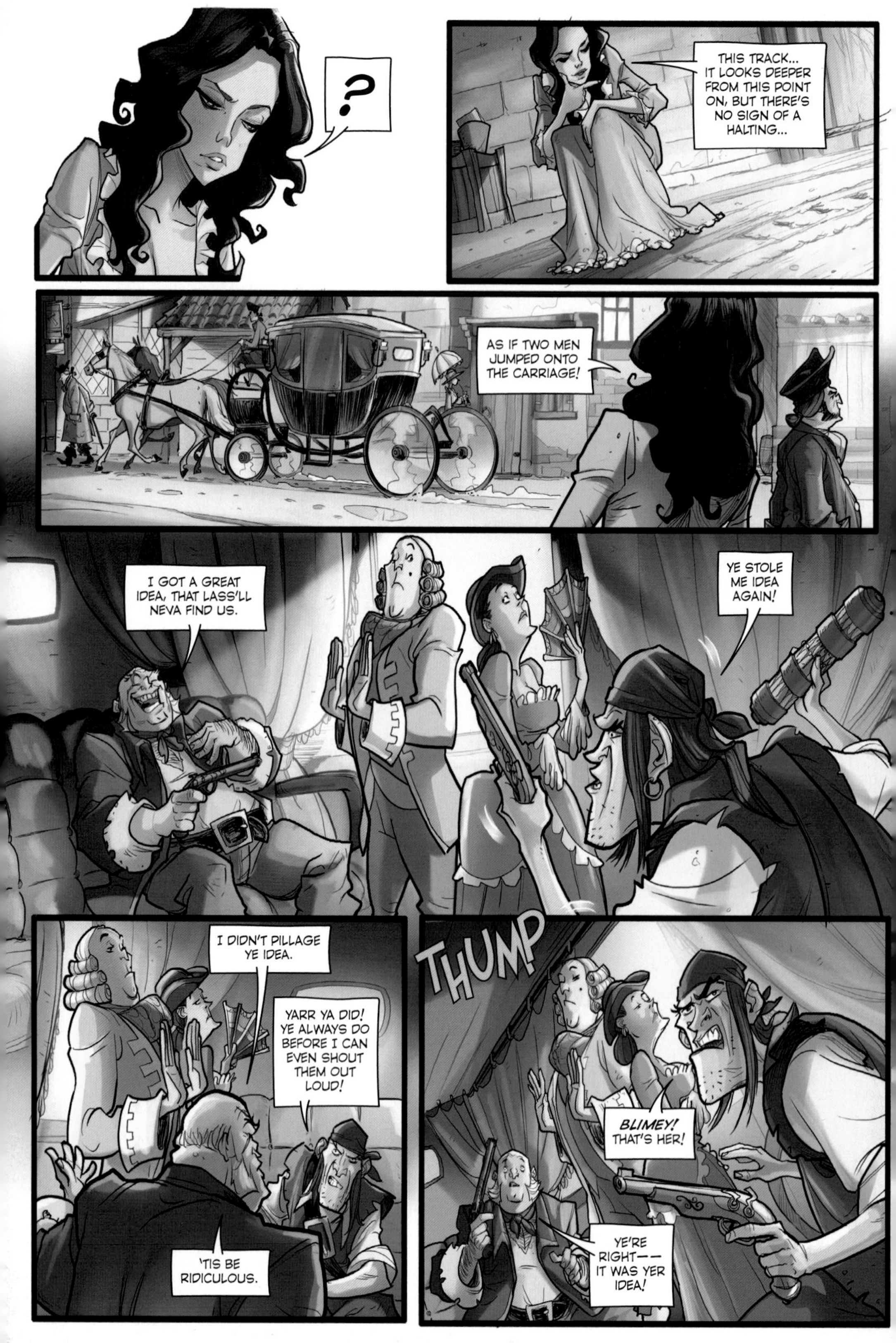
?
THIS TRACK... IT LOOKS DEEPER FROM THIS POINT ON, BUT THERE'S NO SIGN OF A HALTING...
AS IF TWO MEN JUMPED ONTO THE CARRIAGE!
I GOT A GREAT IDEA, THAT LASS'LL NEVA FIND US.
YE STOLE ME IDEA AGAIN!
I DIDN'T PILLAGE YE IDEA.
YARR YA DID! YE ALWAYS DO BEFORE I CAN EVEN SHOUT THEM OUT LOUD!
'TIS BE RIDICULOUS.
THUMP
BLIMEY! THAT'S HER!
YE'RE RIGHT—— IT WAS YER IDEA!

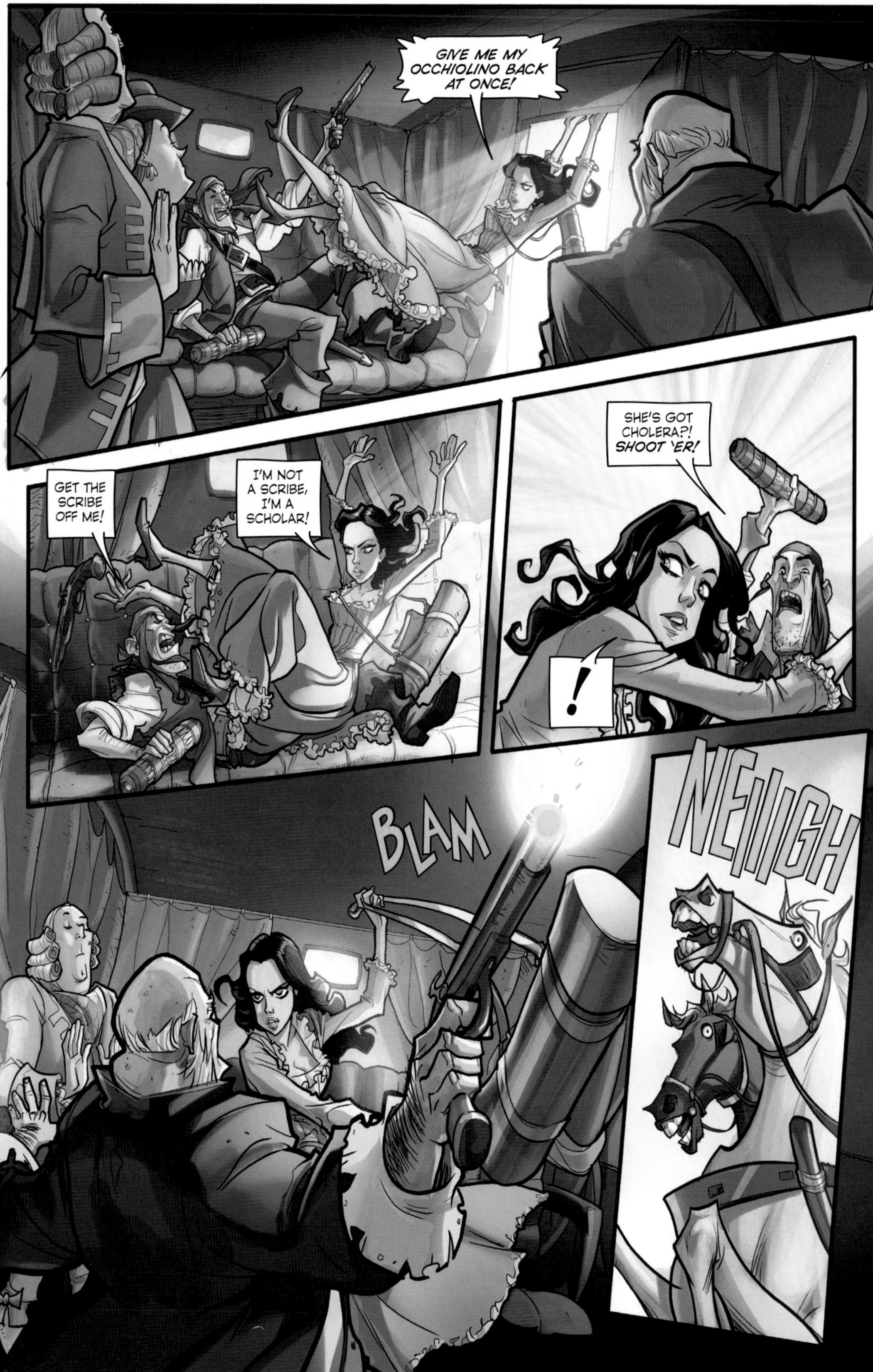
GIVE ME MY OCCHIOLINO BACK AT ONCE!
GET THE SCRIBE OFF ME!
I'M NOT A SCRIBE, I'M A SCHOLAR!
SHE'S GOT CHOLERA?! SHOOT 'ER!
!
BLAM
NEIIIGH

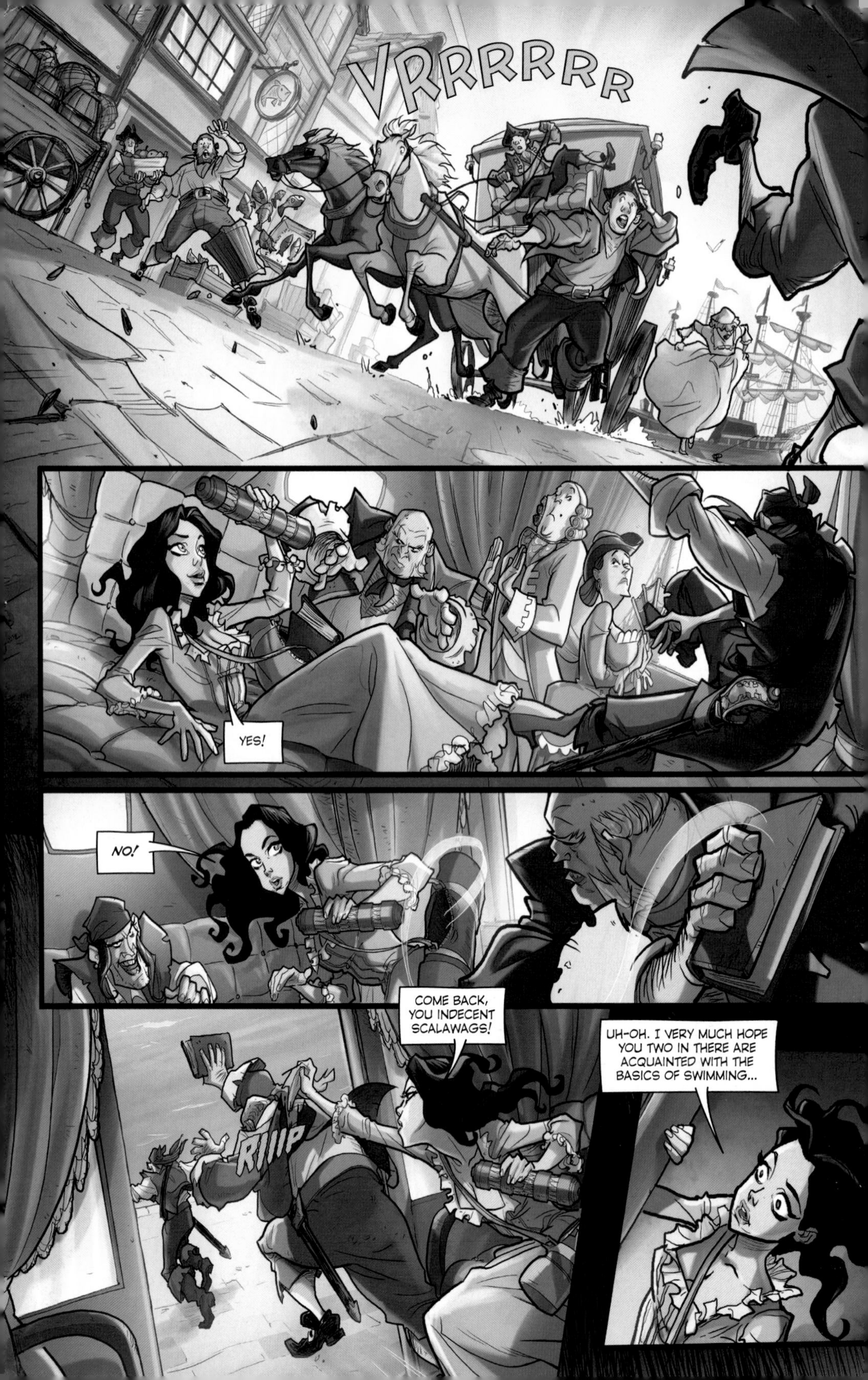
VRRRRRRR
YES!
NO!
COME BACK, YOU INDECENT SCALAWAGS!
RIIIP
UH-OH. I VERY MUCH HOPE YOU TWO IN THERE ARE ACQUAINTED WITH THE BASICS OF SWIMMING...

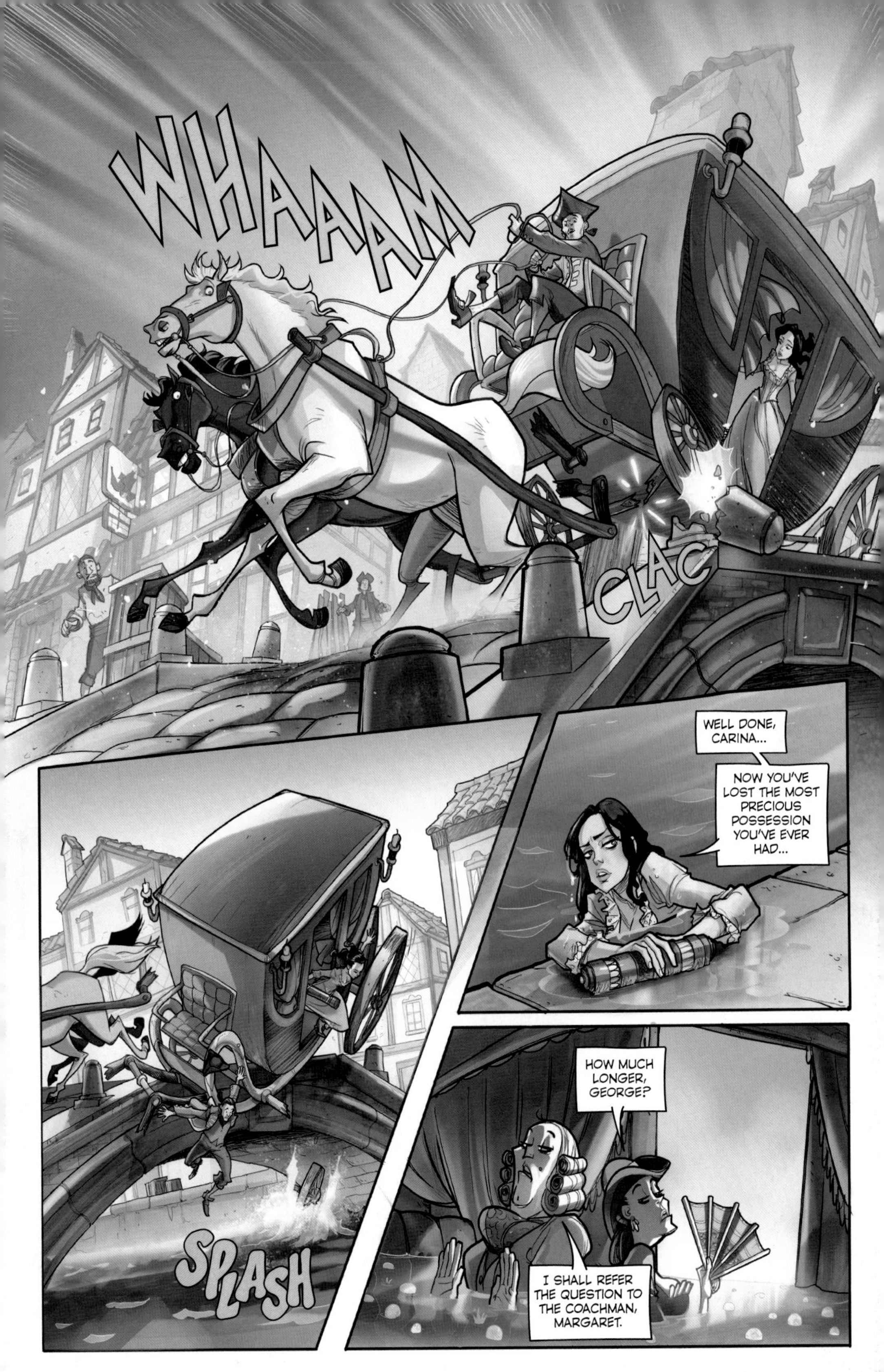
WHAAAM
CLAC
SPLASH
WELL DONE, CARINA...
NOW YOU'VE LOST THE MOST PRECIOUS POSSESSION YOU'VE EVER HAD...
HOW MUCH LONGER, GEORGE?
I SHALL REFER THE QUESTION TO THE COACHMAN, MARGARET.

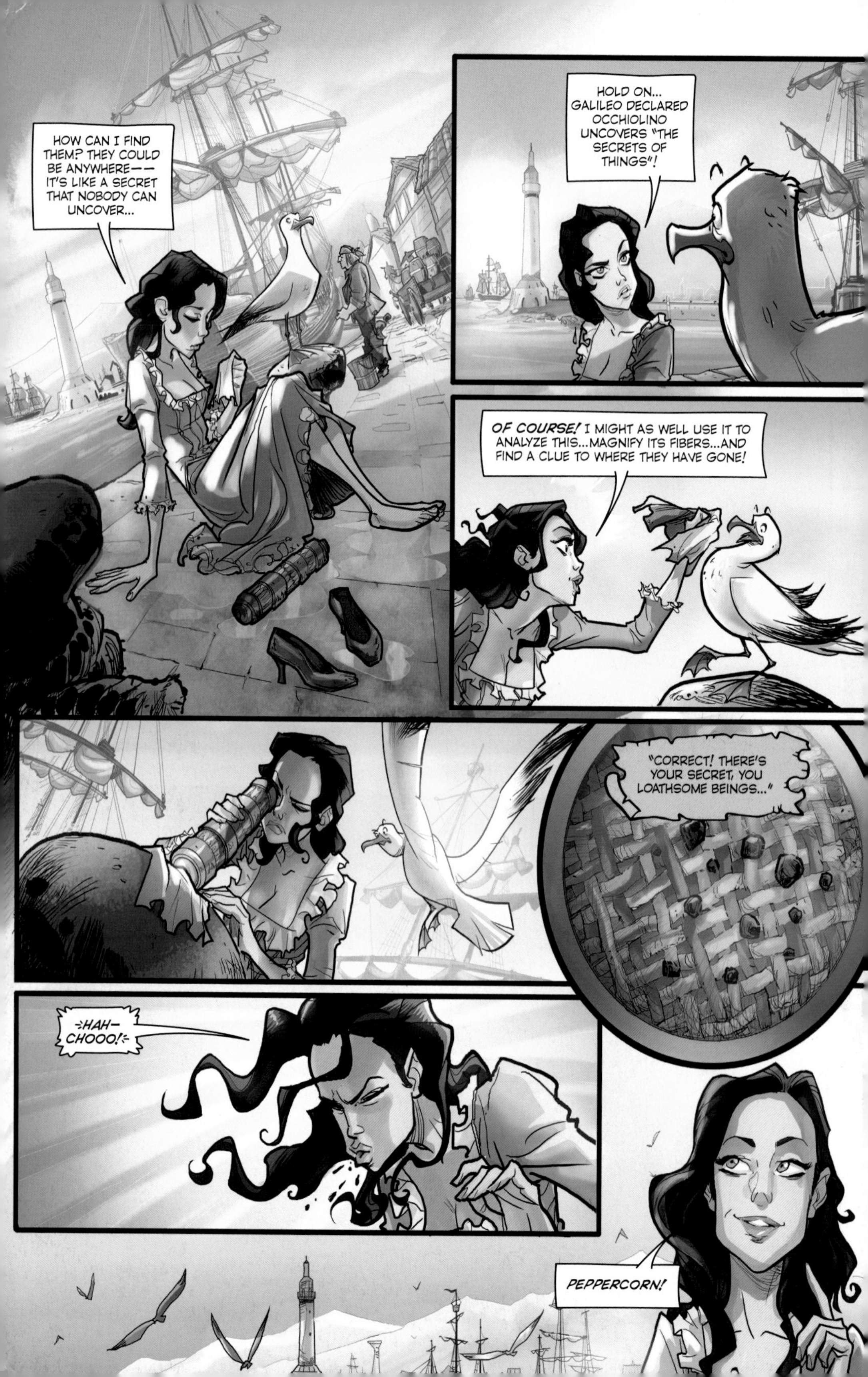
HOW CAN I FIND THEM? THEY COULD BE ANYWHERE-- IT'S LIKE A SECRET THAT NOBODY CAN UNCOVER...
HOLD ON... GALILEO DECLARED OCCHIOLINO UNCOVERS "THE SECRETS OF THINGS"!
OF COURSE! I MIGHT AS WELL USE IT TO ANALYZE THIS...MAGNIFY ITS FIBERS...AND FIND A CLUE TO WHERE THEY HAVE GONE!
"CORRECT! THERE'S YOUR SECRET, YOU LOATHSOME BEINGS..."
HAH-CHOOO!
PEPPERCORN!

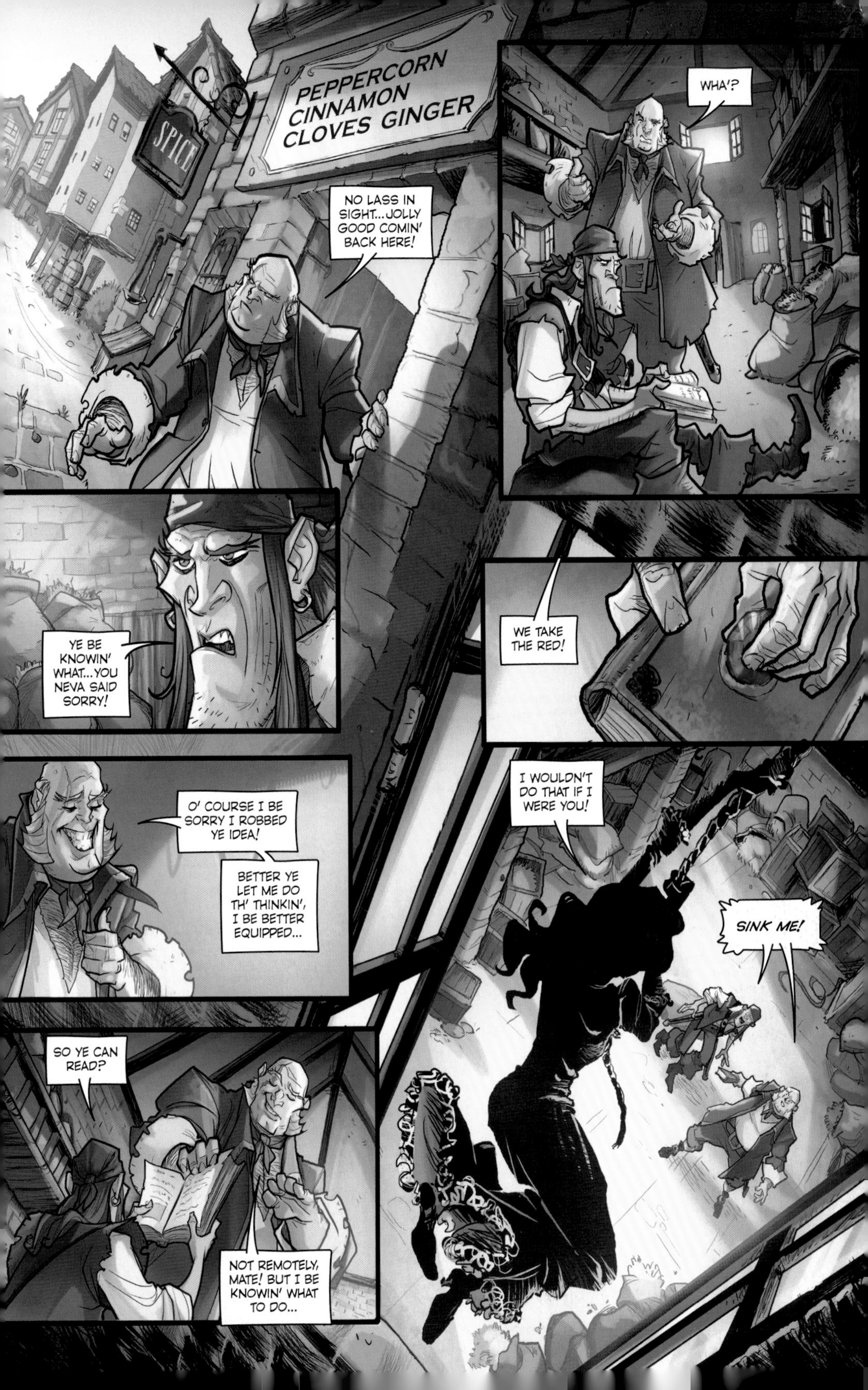
PEPPERCORN CINNAMON CLOVES GINGER
SPICE
NO LASS IN SIGHT...JOLLY GOOD COMIN' BACK HERE!
WHA'?
YE BE KNOWIN' WHAT...YOU NEVA SAID SORRY!
WE TAKE THE RED!
O' COURSE I BE SORRY I ROBBED YE IDEA!
BETTER YE LET ME DO TH' THINKIN', I BE BETTER EQUIPPED...
SO YE CAN READ?
NOT REMOTELY, MATE! BUT I BE KNOWIN' WHAT TO DO...
I WOULDN'T DO THAT IF I WERE YOU!
SINK ME!

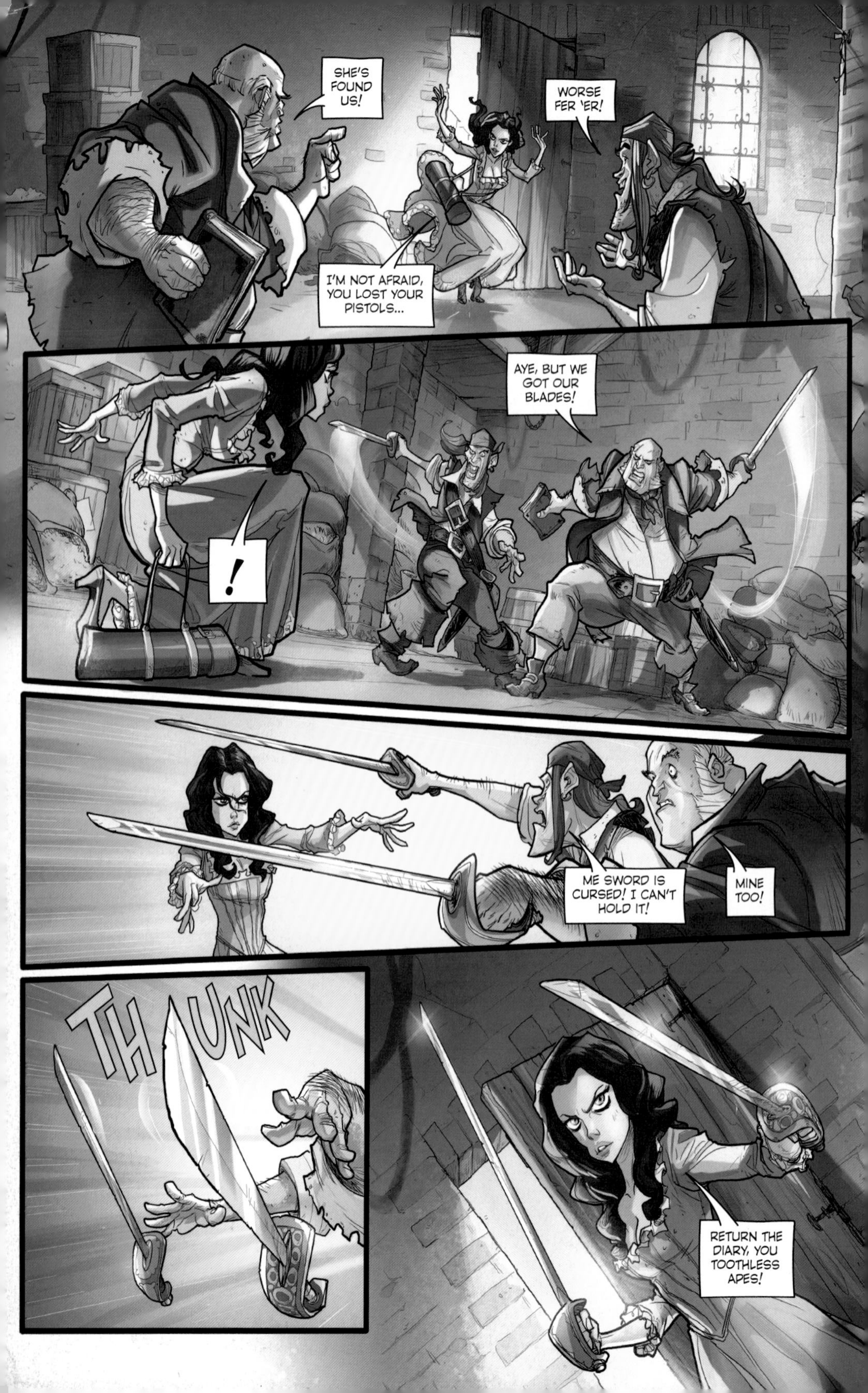

SHE'S FOUND US!
WORSE FER 'ER!
I'M NOT AFRAID, YOU LOST YOUR PISTOLS...
AYE, BUT WE GOT OUR BLADES!
!
ME SWORD IS CURSED! I CAN'T HOLD IT!
MINE TOO!
THUNK
RETURN THE DIARY, YOU TOOTHLESS APES!

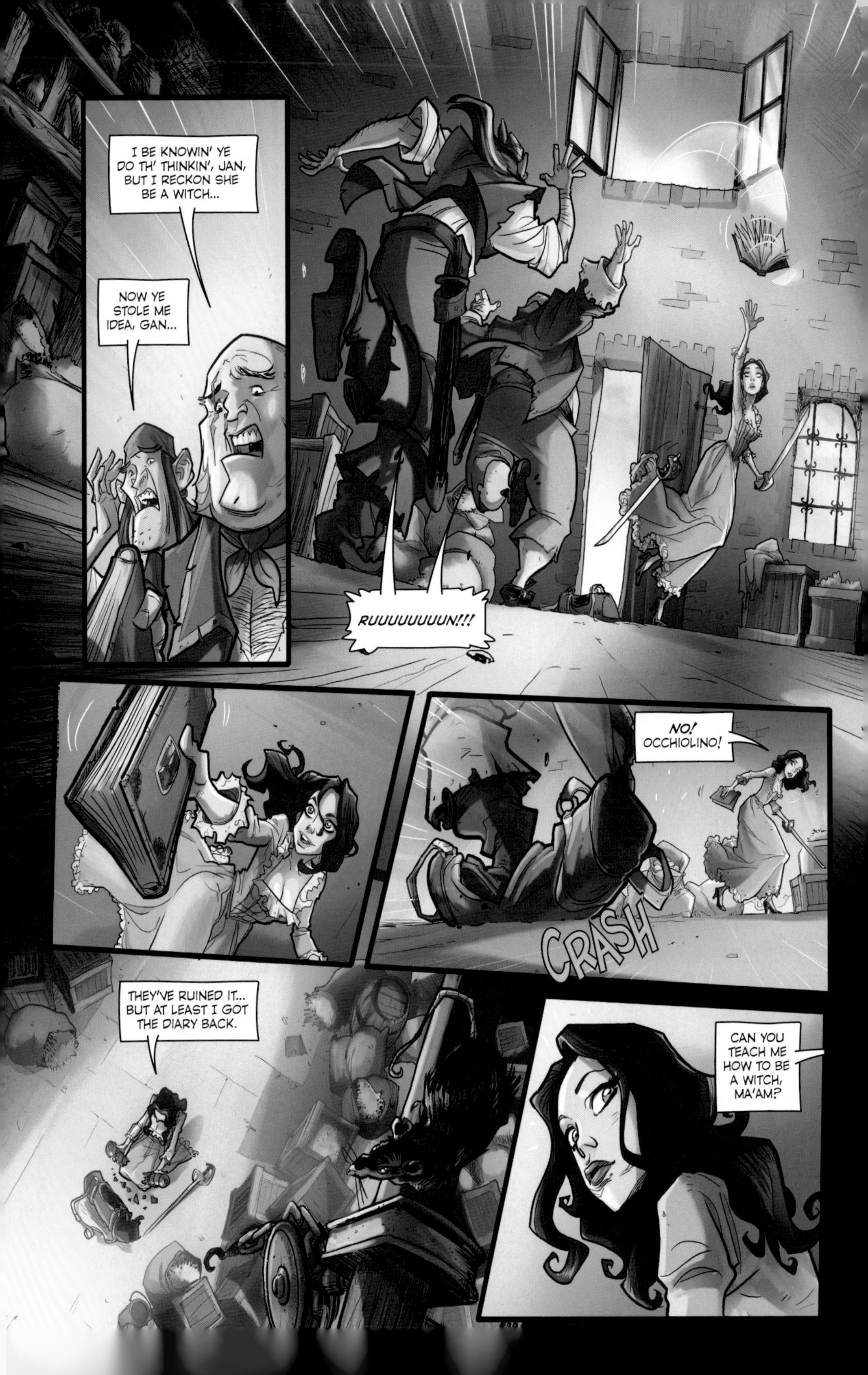
I BE KNOWIN' YE DO TH' THINKIN', JAN, BUT I RECKON SHE BE A WITCH...
NOW YE STOLE ME IDEA, GAN...
RUUUUUUUUN!!!
NO! OCCHIOLINO!
CRASH
THEY'VE RUINED IT... BUT AT LEAST I GOT THE DIARY BACK.
CAN YOU TEACH ME HOW TO BE A WITCH, MA'AM?

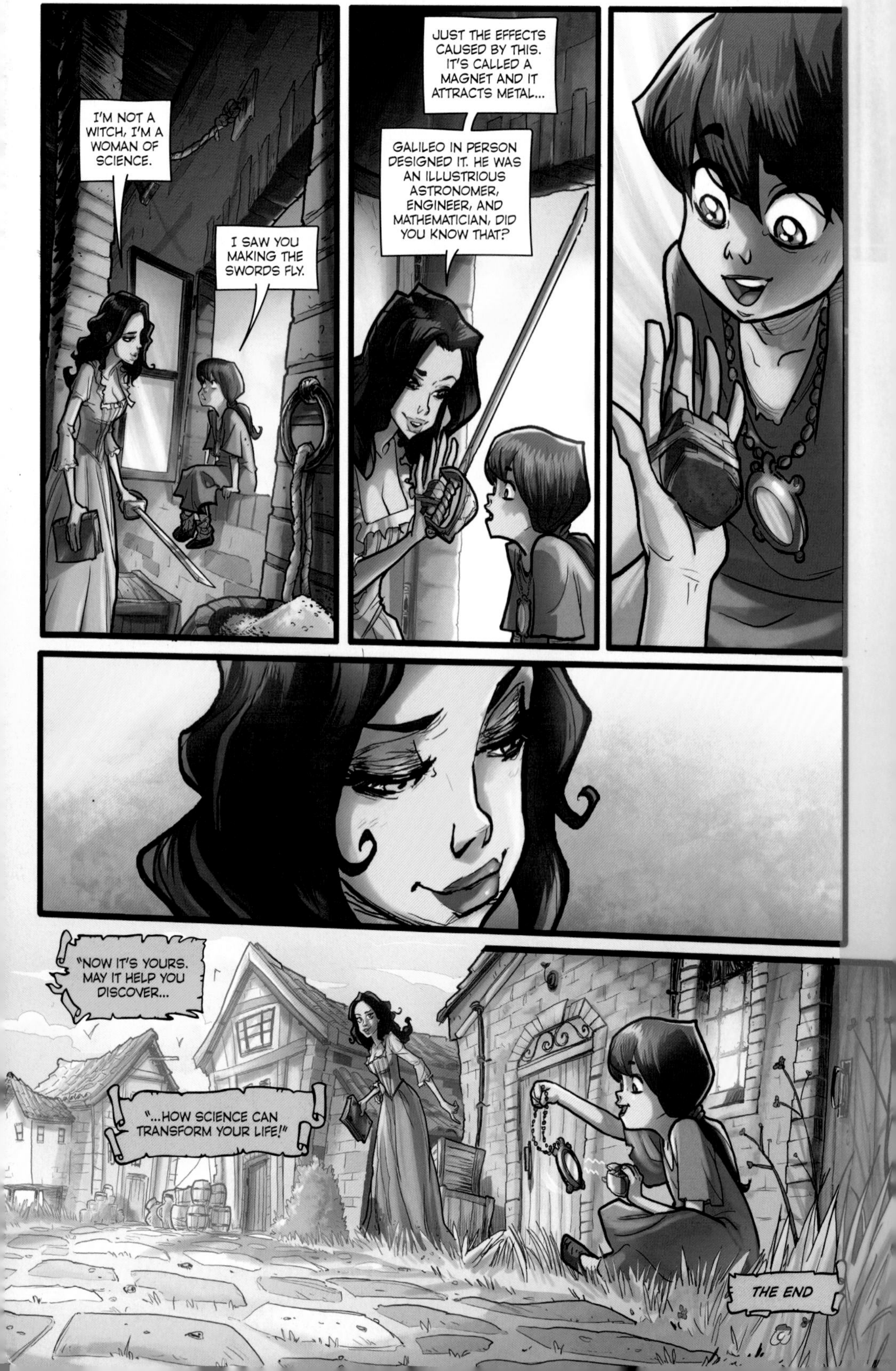
I'M NOT A WITCH, I'M A WOMAN OF SCIENCE.
I SAW YOU MAKING THE SWORDS FLY.
JUST THE EFFECTS CAUSED BY THIS. IT'S CALLED A MAGNET AND IT ATTRACTS METAL...
GALILEO IN PERSON DESIGNED IT. HE WAS AN ILLUSTRIOUS ASTRONOMER, ENGINEER, AND MATHEMATICIAN, DID YOU KNOW THAT?
"NOW IT'S YOURS. MAY IT HELP YOU DISCOVER...
"...HOW SCIENCE CAN TRANSFORM YOUR LIFE!"
THE END

Disney Pirates of the Caribbean: Dead Men Tell No Tales

Movie Graphic Novel

Published simultaneously in the United States and Canada by Joe Books Ltd, 489 College Street, Toronto, ON M6G 1A5

www.joebooks.com

First Joe Books edition: June 2017

Print ISBN: 978-1-77275-525-1
ebook ISBN: 978-1-77275-747-7

Library and Archives Canada Cataloguing in Publication information is available upon request

Printed and bound in Canada
1 3 5 7 9 10 8 6 4 2

THE GRAPHIC NOVEL
SCRIPT ADAPTATION Alessandro Ferrari
LAYOUTS, PENCILS & INKS Giovanni Rigano
CHARACTER DESIGN Igor Chimisso
COLOR Silvano Scolari, Massimo Rocca
LETTERS EDIZIONI BD
ART OPTIMIZATION Ciro Cangialosi

COVER
LAYOUTS & PENCILS Giovanni Rigano
INKS Igor Chimisso
COLOR Slava Panarin

DISNEY PUBLISHING WORLDWIDE
Global Magazines, Comics and Partworks
PUBLISHER Lynn Waggoner
EXECUTIVE EDITOR Stefano Ambrosio
EDITORIAL TEAM Bianca Coletti (Director, Magazines), Guido Frazzini (Director, Comics), Carlotta Quattrocolo (Executive Editor), Camilla Vedove (Senior Manager, Editorial Development), Behnoosh Khalili (Senior Editor), Julie Dorris (Senior Editor)
DESIGN Enrico Soave (Senior Designer), Manny Mederos (Comics & Magazines Creative Manager)
ART Ken Shue (VP, Global Art), Roberto Santillo (Creative Director), Marco Ghiglione (Creative Manager), Stefano Attardi (Computer Art Designer)
PORTFOLIO MANAGEMENT Olivia Ciancarelli (Director)
BUSINESS & MARKETING Mariantonietta Galla (Marketing Manager), Virpi Korhonen (Editorial Manager), Kristen Ginter (Operations Manager)
GRAPHIC DESIGN J-Think.com - Milano
SPECIAL THANKS Dominique Flynn, Dale Kennedy, Jessica Bardwil, Caitlin Dodson.

Copyright © 2017 Disney Enterprises, Inc. All rights reserved.

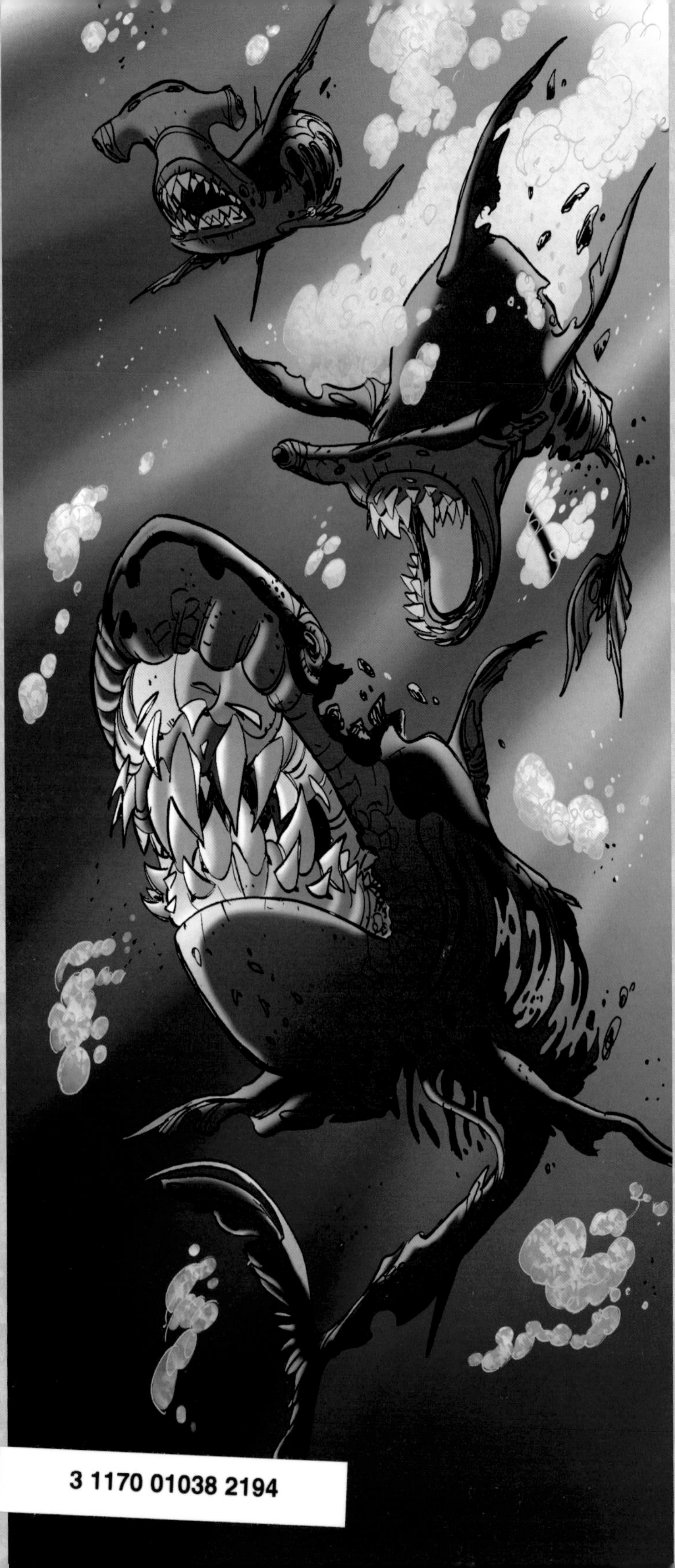